The Risen

ALSO BY RON RASH

FICTION

Above the Waterfall

Something Rich and Strange

The Ron Rash Reader

Nothing Gold Can Stay

The Cove

Burning Bright

Serena

The World Made Straight

Saints at the River

One Foot in Eden

Chemistry and Other Stories

Casualties

The Night the New Jesus Fell to Earth

POETRY

Poems: New and Selected

Waking

Raising the Dead

Among the Believers

Eureka Mill

The Risen

A Novel

Ron Rash

An Imprint of HarperCollinsPublishers

HarperCollins books may be purchased for educational, business, or sales promotional use. For information please e-mail the Special Markets Department at SPsales@harpercollins.com.

FIRST HARPERLUXE EDITION

ISBN: 978-0-06-249709-3

HarperLuxe™ is a trademark of HarperCollins Publishers.

Library of Congress Cataloging-in-Publication Data is available upon request.

16 17 18 19 20   ID/RRD   10 9 8 7 6 5 4 3 2

For George Singleton

And after that the punishment began.

—FYODOR DOSTOYEVSKY
The Brothers Karamazov

She is waiting. Each spring the hard rains come and the creek rises and quickens, and more of the bank peels off, silting the water brown and bringing to light another layer of dark earth. Decades pass. She is patient, shelled inside the blue tarp. Each spring the water laps closer, paling roots, loosening stones, scuffing and smoothing. She is waiting and one day a bit of blue appears in the bank and then more blue. The rain pauses and the sun appears but she is ready now and the bank trembles a moment and heaves and the strands of tarp unfurl and she spills into the stream and is free. Bits of bone gather in an eddy, form a brief necklace. The current moves on toward the sea.

PART ONE

CHAPTER ONE

From the beginning, Ligeia's ability to appear or disappear seemed magical. The first time, forty-six years ago, was at Panther Creek the summer before my junior year in high school. On Sundays after church and a lunch at our grandfather's house, my older brother, Bill, and I changed into T-shirts and cutoff jeans, tossed our fishing gear into the '62 Ford pickup Grandfather had bought us, and headed west out of Sylva. We'd cross the interstate, turn onto national forestland, and drive a mile down the gravel road bordering Panther Creek, rods and reels rattling in the truck bed as Bill veered onto an old logging trail. Soon tree limbs and saplings raked the hood and windshield. Then there was no longer a road, only a gap in the trees through which Bill wove until skidding to a stop.

Only two miles away, the Tuckaseegee River held larger trout and deeper swimming holes, but the trout and pools here were enough for us. Best of all, we had this section of stream to ourselves and wanted to keep it that way, which was why Bill parked where the truck could not be seen from the road. We made our way through a thicket of mountain laurel whose branches sometimes whipped back, marking us with welts and scratches. At the stream, we baited our hooks and cast upstream where the current slowed, forming a wide, deep pool. Bill and I set the rods on rocks, stripped to our cutoff jeans, and swam in the pool's tailwaters. When a rod tip trembled, one of us got out to reel in what tugged the line. Often it was a knottyhead or catfish, but if a trout we gilled it onto our metal stringer. Grandfather enjoyed eating fresh trout and demanded we bring some back. Our mother rolled the fish in cornmeal and fried them for "the old man," as Bill and I sometimes called him, though never to his face.

After hours of wearing stifling suits while seated on rigid pews and high-backed dining chairs, to enter water and splay our limbs was freeing. The midday sun fell full on the pool, so when we waded in up to our waists, heat and cold balanced as if by a carpenter's level. That was the best sensation, knowing in a moment, but not quite yet, I'd dive into cold but emerge into warmth. Years later at Wake Forest, when I still believed I might create literature, I'd write a mediocre poem about those mornings in church and afterward the "baptism of nature."

We'd caught five trout before Bill lifted the fish from the water, signaling it was time to go. Through a gap in the canopy, the declining sun brightened the stringer's silver sheen, flared the red slashes on each trout's flanks. *A sloshing chandelier* was how I described it to my mother that evening. Bill opened the Ka-Bar pocketknife that had once belonged to our father and locked the blade. *Good practice,* he said, given that after his upcoming year at Wake Forest he'd be heading to Bowman Gray, not to be a GP like our grandfather but a surgeon.

I was lifting a beach towel from the sand when I saw her.

"Someone's downstream," I said, "in the pool where the creek bends."

"A fisherman?" Bill asked, and set down the trout he was gutting. The knife remained in his hand as he took a few steps downstream. "I don't see anyone."

"A girl," I said. "She was in the pool, watching us, and then she dove underwater."

"A girl?" Bill asked. "A child or 'girl' like somebody our age?"

"Our age."

"In a swimsuit?"

"I don't think she was wearing anything," I answered.

"Nothing, even on her bottom half?"

"Nothing on the part I could see."

"Was anyone with her?"

"I don't think so."

Bill set the knife on the sand.

"Well, let's go look."

But the pool lay empty, unrippled. No footprints indented the sand.

"You haven't been sneaking into Grandfather's office closet, have you, little brother?" Bill asked.

"She could have gotten out on the other side," I said. On the far bank, surrounded by rhododendron, a granite slab long and wide as a shed door leaned into the stream. I pointed at a damp shadow. "It looks like water dripped on that rock."

"A muskrat or otter could do that," Bill said.

He walked downstream, saw nothing, and went through the woods far enough to scan the gravel road.

"I don't see a vehicle," Bill said when he came back. "So where did she come from, Eugene? Is she a mermaid who swam up from the Atlantic?"

"Someone might have dropped her off, or she could have come over the ridge. There are houses there."

"Houses, not a nudist colony." Bill laid a hand on my shoulder, firm enough that I couldn't shrug it off. "We've got to get you a real girl so you won't be dreaming one up."

"Okay, forget it. I was wrong," I said, tired of the teasing but also wondering if maybe I had imagined her.

But I hadn't, and now, all of these years later, Ligeia has, once again, suddenly appeared, though this time not at Panther Creek but on the front page of our county newspaper, and looking no older than she did in 1969. A mermaid who hadn't returned to the ocean after all, which is why I've broken my rule about drinking before five P.M. It is morning but an empty pint of Jack Daniel's lies on the coffee table beside last night's wine bottle. An hour ago I'd read the headline "Remains Identified as Jane Mosely," refolded the newspaper, and set it facedown on the couch. Now I hope the whiskey buffers me enough to read the whole article. *I crawled into that whiskey bottle and stayed there.* Years ago, I'd heard those words on a Friday evening in the Sylva Methodist Church basement. I'd never thought of whiskey that way before, but it is what you seek—to be suspended in that amber glow. Seek but not always achieve, because this morning I can't find my way to that place.

Bill's office opens at nine. When the stove clock's minute hand reaches its apex, I dial. The receptionist tells me my brother is in surgery.

"When will he get out?" I ask.

"It's an emergency operation, Mr. Matney, so I can't be sure."

"Have him call me as soon as he returns."

"I will make a note of it," the receptionist says.

"Does he have a cell phone or pager?"

"Your brother doesn't answer calls during surgery, Mr. Matney."

"You can at least leave him a message to call me, or give me the number and let me do it myself."

For a few moments the line is silent.

"I will text him," she huffs.

Someone at the hospital might know when Bill would finish, but I'd not be told over the phone. I'm not hungry, but eating gives me something to do while waiting, so I force down a bowl of cereal. Besides, alcohol and an empty stomach are never good. Never.

CHAPTER TWO

That summer Bill and I worked in our grandfather's office weekdays from ten thirty to six, nine to noon Saturdays. We ran errands or answered the phone if Shirley, who served as both nurse and receptionist, was busy or at lunch, which left plenty of time to read books brought from home or the magazines scattered around the reception room. *On call*, our grandfather said, which also meant under his control. When Grandfather and Shirley left at five, Bill and I swept and mopped the floors, cleaned bathrooms and emptied wastebaskets, disinfected the counters and examination tables. The only strenuous work occurred on Saturdays when we waxed and buffed the floors. Since the office was closed, we had the place mostly to ourselves. Holding tight to the buffer as it skittered across the floor was like controlling a lawn mower on ice. Bill and I took fifteen-minute shifts, my arms gelid by the time it was done. Afterward, we'd rest briefly in the waiting room with the air conditioning blasting, then lock the door and enter the midday heat.

During the school year, Nebo, our grandfather's mute handyman, did the office cleaning, but come summer he did yard work, as well as fixing leaky faucets, nailing down loose boards, painting, and whatever else Grandfather ordered him to do. On Saturdays while Bill and I worked inside, Nebo cut the office yard with an old side-wheel mower our grandfather refused to replace. Two or three times each Saturday, the mower blades paused and Nebo came inside for a drink of water but also to inspect our work, always pointing out any spot missed.

The salaries we received equaled that of more taxing jobs, such as working on a city grounds crew or at the local sawmill. Grandfather's hiring Bill and me seemed further assurance of what he'd told our mother when the hunting accident left her a widow—that she and Bill and I would be taken care of. Grandfather owned the house we lived in and let us stay there rent free, all taxes and utilities paid. Our college would be paid for, braces and clothes, whatever other needs. As for the summer jobs, Grandfather could have given us the money outright, but as he told us, it was his duty to instill in us a sense of discipline and responsibility. The jobs fulfilled another purpose though—to keep Bill focused on becoming a surgeon. The office's medical environment helped with that, but the work also kept Bill close to Sylva and away from Virginia, where his girlfriend, Leslie, was home from Wake Forest for the summer.

That Bill would become a surgeon had been decreed when he was still in elementary school. "Look at how he trims the fat off that roast," Grandfather told our mother. "A natural-born surgeon and destined to be one of the best, just as I and his father would have been. And you, Eugene," my grandfather added, smiling as he turned to me, "you're not even using the correct hand. I don't know of a single left-handed surgeon. Southpaws see things differently, which isn't what you want from someone wielding a scalpel. It would not matter so much as a GP, but your mother insists on directing you toward more artistic pursuits." For one of the few times I ever witnessed, our mother openly disagreed with her father-in-law. "No," she'd replied quietly, "I merely wish my sons to follow their own interests."

Grandfather's attempts to shape our futures had started even earlier. The first Christmas present I remember was a black plastic doctor's bag filled with a toy stethoscope and thermometer, a rubber hammer to test reflexes, and plastic scalpels much like picnic knives. There were children's books about medicine, plastic human models with organs and veins. Early on, Grandfather took Bill to the office and on house calls for patients too elderly to leave home. Bill later claimed there wasn't ever a time that he hadn't thought of becoming a surgeon. But how could it have been otherwise?

Our grandfather continued to encourage me to think about a medical career, but only halfheartedly. I occasionally went to his office and on patient visits. If he showed Bill something under his microscope or explained a diagnosis, he might include me, perhaps thinking I might yet become one of the elect. Or perhaps it was a way to diminish my mother's influence. But once Bill declared premed at Wake Forest, my grandfather never mentioned medicine to me again.

After Bill's teasing about mermaids, the following Sunday I'd decided to stay home and read.

"Bring your book and come with me, Eugene," he insisted. "I'll lay off the mermaid crap and buy us some Pepsis to drink. All you'll have to do is swim and read. I'll tend the fishing lines."

"All right," I finally said.

When we arrived, I laid my towel on the sand and was about to open my paperback when Bill spoke.

"So she is real."

Downstream, the girl I'd seen last week waded in the pool's shallows, though this time she wore a green two-piece bathing suit. If she'd seen us, she wasn't acting like it.

"Do you recognize her?" Bill asked.

"No."

"She fills out that bathing suit nicely, don't you think?" Bill said. "Maybe we should go introduce ourselves."

"I don't know if that's such a good idea. Maybe she wants to be by herself."

"Well, if she does, so be it, but it won't hurt to find out," Bill said, and as always, he led and I followed.

She saw us coming and plunged into the deeper water.

"Hey," Bill shouted. "We just wanted to introduce ourselves."

We'd run her off again, I figured, but when we got to the pool, she was on the stream's opposite side. Her arms lay languidly on the rock shelf, head and shoulders out of the water, the green bikini top just under the surface. Her long red hair set off her aqua eyes and unblemished complexion. Close up, she looked younger, closer to my age than Bill's. Bright beads circled her neck. *Love beads*, I knew they were called. Affixed to the beads was a penny-size peace symbol. She raised a hand and tucked her dripping hair behind her ears, exposing a pale crescent of breast. I looked away, feeling my face flush.

"What do you guys want?" she asked.

Her accent was that of the Floridians whose second homes dotted the nearby ridges.

"Just to say hello. I'm Bill and this is my brother, Eugene."

She sank lower in the water, up to the necklace, all the while her eyes on us.

"You're not from around here, are you?" Bill asked.

"No, but I can tell you are," she said, nodding at our cutoff jeans. "Did those used to be overalls?"

"We're not hicks," Bill said, his face reddening. "I'm a senior at Wake Forest and we live in Sylva, not out here. Our grandfather, he's a doctor."

"Hey, don't get so uptight. I was just joking," she said, then added in the same cool tone. "This grandfather of yours, is his office in Sylva?"

"Yes."

"I can dig that," she said.

"So where are you from?" Bill asked.

"Florida, Daytona Beach."

"Are you here on vacation?"

"Only if you call being bored out of my damn mind for a whole summer a vacation."

"So your family has a second home up here?" Bill asked, and when she didn't answer, "How'd you get to the stream? I mean, did someone drop you off?"

"Can your brother talk?" she asked.

"Yes," Bill said, turning to me.

"What's your name?" I stammered.

"Ligeia."

"That's a nice name," I said. "I've never known anyone called that before."

"That's the kind of name I wanted," she said, "not some moldy old name like Jane."

"Eugene saw you last week," Bill said, and grinned. "He thought you might be a mermaid."

"I did not," I said, my face flushing yet again.

"Maybe I am one," Ligeia said, looking only at me. "You haven't checked out my bottom half yet, right?"

"I didn't mean to do that," I mumbled, "to see you, I mean."

For a few moments no one spoke. Ligeia closed her eyes and eased under the water and then came back up. She ran a flat palm over her brow and opened her eyes wide, as if surprised that we were still there.

"If you want, you can come up to where we are," Bill said. "It's a bigger pool."

"We've got some cold Pepsis," I added.

"Drinking Pepsis," Ligeia asked, "is that what you call a happening around here?"

"A happening?" I asked.

"A party, a good time," Ligeia said, and looked at Bill. "You're old enough to buy alcohol legal like, aren't you?"

"Yes."

"And you haven't got anything stronger than Pepsi?"

"No," Bill answered. "I mean, not with us."

"Then I'll hang out here."

"Next time we could," Bill said. "I'll buy some beer."

"I hate the taste of beer," Ligeia said. "What about some whiskey, or pot?"

"If I was at school I could get whiskey," Bill said, "but around here . . ."

"But there's an ABC store in town?"

"Yeah, but buying some there wouldn't be a good idea," Bill answered, leaving it at that.

"Can you at least score a bottle of Strawberry Hill?" Ligeia asked. "It's like drinking Kool-Aid but I can get it down."

"I can get that," Bill said.

Ligeia gazed past us a few moments, then looked down and touched the beads with her index finger, tracing them back and forth along the front of her neck. She resettled her forearms on the rock and looked at us.

"You guys hang out at your grandfather's office much?"

"We work there, cleaning up mainly," I said.

"I bet there's plenty of sample packs laying around, something to mellow us out, like some Quaaludes or Valium. Bring some of those and I'll show you how we party in the Sunshine State." Ligeia paused and smiled. "Like your little brother saw last week, I can let it all hang out."

There is no way we're doing anything like that, I expected Bill to say, but instead he asked Ligeia's age.

"How old do I look?"

"Eugene's sixteen," Bill answered. "I'd guess you're at least a year older, maybe two."

"I think I'll keep you guessing about that and if I have feet or fins," Ligeia said. "Some mystery always makes a chick more interesting, right?"

"What time will you be here on Sunday?" I asked.

"I'm here when I appear," Ligeia answered.

She swam into the shadowy water beside the ledge, gave us a wink, and slowly sank. As her head disappeared, the long red hair fanned out on the surface.Then, like a night flower closing, it regathered and was gone.

"Come on," Bill said, and we walked back to our pool. I reeled in the line to check the bait.

"Sounds like skinny dipping may be involved when they party in Florida," Bill said.

"Last week, she didn't know we were here," I answered. "She's wearing a bathing suit now that she knows someone else is around."

"You don't wear a bathing suit top like that unless you want to be looked at, little brother, though she could be like those summer girls at the pool. They want us to look so they can act stuck up like their parents."

"I don't think she's like them," I answered. "Her accent is but her words aren't. They are more like, you know . . ."

"Like a hippie would use," Bill said.

"She looks like one, the love beads and all."

"Or pretending to be one, just to act like she's cooler than us," Bill said. "There are a couple of guys at Wake Forest who do that. They were jerks before they grew their hair out and they're still jerks."

"I don't think she's a jerk."

"No," Bill said, "but I hope she doesn't get sick this summer. Can you imagine how the old man would react? Those beads with the peace sign alone would send him into orbit. I'm just glad he's so pumped up on my becoming a surgeon. Otherwise, he'd say screw the high lottery number, you're going over there anyway." Bill paused, his voice mockingly stentorian. "You learn responsibility in war, boy."

"He'd be glad to send me," I said, "even if my number was three hundred and sixty-five."

"Mom wouldn't let that happen," Bill said, and paused. "I wouldn't either."

A rod dipped and I reeled in a catfish. I picked it up carefully, avoiding the spiny fin that could slice a palm open. I freed the hook and threw the fish back into the pool.

"We're coming back next week, aren't we?" I asked. Bill nodded.

"She's right," he said, "some whiskey would be nice."

"There's no way Mr. Jenson will sell it to you."

"I know," Bill said, "but if her parents are like most of these Florida folks, they have a well-stocked liquor cabinet. I bet she could sneak some out if she tried, at least enough for a couple of drinks, which is all we need anyway. I'm going to go ask her."

But when we went downstream, Ligeia was gone.

"Let's wait a few minutes before leaving," Bill said. "I want to see who picks her up."

We loaded up the truck, turned it around to face the gravel road.

"Where did she disappear to?" Bill asked after twenty minutes. "This road's a dead end. There's nothing after that but forestland."

"Like I told you last week, she may have come from over the ridge. They could have a place on Chestnut Road."

"Maybe so," Bill mused. "When's the last time you were up there?"

"A couple of years ago."

"I haven't been since high school. Back then it was nothing but trailers and farmhouses."

"You know how those second homes are," I said. "They can cover a ridge quick as kudzu."

"Nice simile. Save that for one of your poems," Bill said, cranking the truck. We bumped up the skid trail onto the gravel. "You know, little brother, being the shy sensitive artist only works on girls if they *know* you are shy and sensitive. If you just stare at them with your mouth open, they think you're like Nebo. *Comprende?*"

"Ligeia's interested in you, not me."

"Well, she didn't seem to be playing favorites, and if you're her type, then good for you. After all, I've got Leslie, though she could just as well be on the moon this summer."

"What about getting some samples out of Grandfather's closet?" I asked.

"I'm still thinking about that," Bill said as we turned onto the four-lane. "It's not like he'd miss one sample. Those shelves are packed with more meds than the drugstore. And he and Shirley won't be there on Saturday. But of course Nebo will be and you know how he is. Even if he's not working he'll hang around and check up on us."

"I know," I agreed.

"But it's not like he can see through walls, right? As long as he's outside, there's no reason to worry."

But I did worry. Like every child in Sylva, I'd grown up terrified of Nebo. He was over six feet tall, wiry, but with huge hands and a shaved head. He never wore a hat or cap, so in summer his skull reddened as if dipped in boiling water. He had to be, like Grandfather, in his early seventies, but Nebo was strong enough to carry a trash-filled fifty-five-gallon steel barrel to the curbside each Wednesday. But most unsettling was his silence. Nebo had arrived in Sylva a day after Grandfather returned from World War One, and he'd immediately moved into our grandfather's guesthouse. The timing made many in town assume they'd met during the war, and that Grandfather had perhaps saved his life. There were no visible scars on Nebo but he walked with an odd gait, one leg half a beat behind the other. Some believed his muteness, like his hacking cough, had been caused by mustard gas.

Nebo occasionally worked for others, chopping wood, painting, but only with Grandfather's permission. As if more golem than handyman, he waited between jobs on the office's back porch steps, in one hand a long straight razor and in the other a whetstone. You could hear the breathlike rasping and, when he raised the blade to inspect the edge, see the honed steel blaze in the sunlight. His doing so precipitated more than a few children's nightmares, including some of my own. And no doubt some adult nightmares as well, I suspect now, because Nebo had been present the December day in 1918 when our grandfather confronted the salesman. Many in town believed that later the same evening, the salesman's final appointment was with Nebo.

"I can buy some beer and wine at that store," Bill said as we passed a convenience store on the four-lane. "This far out of town Grandfather won't find out, especially from a guy who hardly speaks English."

"I think so too," I agreed, "unless one of Grandfather's patients is in there at the same time."

"Yeah, I'd need to be careful about that," Bill said, but then he slapped an open palm against the dashboard. "Damn it, I'm of age, so even if he does find out . . . But he won't," my brother said less harshly, giving me a glance. "So, little brother, are you a Pabst Blue Ribbon guy or into the fancy stuff like Heineken?"

"I don't know," I answered.

"Come on, Eugene," Bill chuckled. "Don't tell me that you haven't sneaked a few beers."

"No, I haven't."

"Not even one?"

"No."

"What in the hell do you do all the time?" Bill asked incredulously. "You can't read and write every minute. You don't play sports or date or go to movies. At least I figured you'd drink. Has there ever been a writer who *didn't* drink?"

I've passed out in my chair and can't get to the phone until the sixth ring. It's not my brother but a telemarketer guaranteeing 25 percent off my car insurance. Not likely, I think. I check the stove's clock and delete an hour because I don't switch to daylight savings time. I want five o'clock to stay five o'clock. I dial the number again and get a recording that the office closes between noon and two. I could drive the fifty miles to Asheville, but there's too much alcohol in me to risk it. So I wait in the front room, the newspaper on the couch, the front page still facedown. The little buffering the whiskey gave me has drained away and I feel the house's hollowness. People don't have to be dead to be ghosts, I think as I stare at the mantel. Except for one, the photos are dusty and light faded, but still discernible: Bill and I dressed for Easter. Another of Bill in his high school baseball uniform and, beside it, one of me at my Beta Club induction. To the left, my mother and father on their wedding day. And one more—my daughter Sarah's photograph, the sole proof in this house that I once had a family. There is no scar above Sarah's left eye because this is her tenth-grade class picture, taken two months before the accident. No photograph of my grandfather is on the mantel, nor ever has been, one of the rare opportunities my mother had to keep his presence outside our lives.

I will have my say in their upbringing, Grandfather told our mother. He always checked our report cards and when Bill made his one B in high school, the old man declared there'd be no med school unless Bill "did his part." My two junior-year-end B's in Chemistry I and French III brought threats that if I didn't get into Wake Forest, by then his, my father's, and my brother's alma mater, he'd not pay for me to go elsewhere. Clothes, length of hair, where we could or could not go, Grandfather made those decisions.

But our mother had a subversive streak. For years she read to us every night, though she sensed early on that Bill, by temperament as much as Grandfather's influence, had little interest in what existed only in the imagination. She made sure our bedroom book-shelves held as much fiction as nonfiction. Twain and Poe and London, then Hemingway and Steinbeck. She loved nineteenth-century novels, especially Austen and Dickens, but the book she cherished most was *Look Homeward, Angel,* a novel set just fifty miles from Sylva. *I suppose it was selfish on my part encourag-ing you toward literature,* my mother told me her last week alive, *but it was as if your grandfather wished to erase any part of me in the both of you. He was a hard, intolerant man, overly pragmatic too, as such men almost always are. I wanted you and your brother to see there could be more within you, much more. And I succeeded, you first but eventually Bill too, though of course Leslie deserves more credit than I do. And yet,* my mother said, *if you had gone into medicine, your life . . .*

My mother had stopped there, the only sounds the beeps and wheezes of machines measuring her ebbing life. When I asked if she wanted me to read more Wolfe or Austen, my mother nodded no and closed her eyes for a few minutes. It had exhausted her, this speaking of matters not spoken of before. A final act of tidying up, much the same as she'd made sure the house was swept and mopped, counters cleared of clutter, before leaving to enter the hospital—that is how I've come to view those last days I spent with her. But she knew some things cannot be tidied up.

That's what novels so often get wrong, knowingly get wrong, my mother had said when she reopened her eyes. *You make certain choices and you leave life never knowing if they were right or wrong. When your father died, I didn't know how to go on. I knew raising Bill and you without him would be harder, but what I couldn't bear was how much I missed your father. I couldn't escape that feeling, not even for a few minutes. I loved him that much. At night when you and Bill were in bed, I'd cry myself to sleep. When Bill was at school and you were napping, I'd cry then too. There were mornings my body felt such a gray heaviness, I could barely rise from the bed, and I kept thinking,* Tomorrow will be better, *but it wasn't. So one day I told myself that I must act as though your father was never in my life, that I wouldn't look at pictures of him or read letters he'd written me. I wouldn't talk about him, and if someone else did, I'd change the subject. I talked about him to you and Bill but never told you of how much I loved him and how much I missed him, or how much of your father I saw in you and Bill. I feared if I spoke of it, especially to you two, I'd never be able to hold the loss in again. I'd lie in bed and never get up. But now I believe perhaps I should have, that the worst thing was not speaking of how much I loved him, because even though your father was no longer alive, you'd know the love that brought you into this world was still alive in me, and so a part of him had not died.*

When I'd reminded my mother that she had told me of that love on a rainy day in Asheville, she'd replied, *Yes, and maybe too late, and not to Bill, only you.* Maybe you were right not to have spoken of it before, I'd said. If you had been overcome by it, unable to leave bed, Bill and I would have been raised by Grandfather. *Yes, but we'll never know, will we?* my mother responded, and nodded at the copy of *Pride and Prejudice* by her bedside. *Austen knew these things. She understood why we need art.*

Yet my mother was only partly correct about our not knowing. There are some choices you make and you do know, ever afterward, to your last breath—of course, these are only the wrong ones.

"Dr. Matney's already with his first patient," the receptionist tells me when I dial Bill's office at 2:05.

"But you gave him my message?"

"Yes, Mr. Matney, I did."

"Tell him I need to talk now."

"He is with a patient, Mr. Matney," the receptionist says, more brusquely.

"The patient can wait."

"I will tell him *after* he's finished with the patient."

I hang the phone back on its wall mount. I'm one of the last people in the county without a cell phone or a computer, because I have no need for them. I keep the landline only in hopes of one day picking up the phone and hearing my daughter's voice.

CHAPTER THREE

When I was three and Bill eight, our father fell from a tree stand while hunting in Tennessee. He died during an emergency operation in the county's hospital. A botched surgery, Grandfather always claimed, though what, if anything, he based this on I never knew. At the time, we lived in Asheville, where my father was finishing up his residency. Our mother had grown up in Winston-Salem and she may have wished to return there to be near her family, but Grandfather convinced her to stay in Sylva. My mother's relatives, all textile workers, could provide little of what he offered.

She was the first in her family to get a college degree, and it had not been easy. The lines of A's on her high school report cards drew the resentment of other mill-village kids. Once she was at Greensboro College, extra jobs paid for what scholarships did not. Her first roommate made snide comments about her closet filled with bare hangers; her second offered hand-me-downs, which my mother said was worse. But in her junior year she met my father at a social, and they married during his first semester of medical school.

Perhaps it was always about loving my father, but how could my mother not have been relieved to know that by marrying a doctor she'd never have to scratch and claw for anything again. *There's nothing ennobling about being poor*, she'd once told me. *I've done what I can to keep you and your brother from learning that firsthand.* And then there she was, a widow with two young sons. With an English degree from Greensboro, she could teach, but with Bill and me to raise it would mean teetering bank accounts and past-due bills, what she had known growing up but wanted to spare her children. Is it ungenerous to believe that she accepted her father-in-law's offer as much for herself as her sons? I don't think so. Only once, when Bill was thirteen and I eight, did our mother tell us to pack our belongings. We were leaving Sylva to live in Winston-Salem, she'd said. But we didn't leave.

Grandfather never spoke negatively to Bill and me about our mother's background. He admired her determination, her "grit" in bettering herself. She knew what she had to do and she'd done it, he told Bill and me. Now, as his son's widow, she need do nothing more than stay home and raise his two grandsons. Or be allowed to, I later realized, for when Grandfather died during my junior year at Wake Forest, my mother altered her life radically. My grandfather had willed the house to her and enough money to live comfortably, but he was barely in the ground when she began working part-time at the library and then full-time. She soon was dating a retired high school guidance counselor, which made me believe that part of Grandfather's pact with her included not seeking a second husband.

You make choices in life and you must accept the consequences of those choices. Bill and I had heard Grandfather's maxim often growing up, occasioned by everything from a toothache to a low grade. War confirmed this view, he said, and told us of a fellow soldier whose falling asleep on guard duty allowed a German to get close enough to toss a grenade in their trench. Three men in the squadron died and Grandfather lost half of two fingers, which, being on his right hand, ensured that he'd forever be a GP. None of the other soldiers spoke to that man in the days afterward, Grandfather claimed, even after he'd begged forgiveness and vowed it would never happen again. Ten days later during a counterattack, mustard gas canisters landed in their unit's midst. The sleeping guard clamped on his mask, only to find the hose severed. He'd lost his sight and his lungs were cindered. It took a week for him to die. Which was as it should be, our grandfather told us, since it allowed the lesson to be thoroughly learned. Grandfather never said he'd cut the hose, but he did tell us that the other lesson war had taught him was how easy it was to kill a human being.

As I too almost learned.

She will probably walk with a slight limp the rest of her life, but all in all you should consider yourselves lucky. Another half inch and her femoral artery would have been cut. Then nothing could have saved her. We had been outside Sarah's hospital room, the orthopedic surgeon, Kay, and me. Kay had gasped and raised a hand to her mouth. When I placed a hand lightly, tentatively, on her shoulder, Kay flinched at my touch. I looked into her eyes and what I'd seen there for months—anger, sadness, concern—was gone. She simply looked *through* me, and into a future where I didn't exist.

It's five thirty when the phone finally rings. I'm three shots into the whiskey, quickening my search for the glow first felt on a Sunday at Panther Creek.

"I know why you've been calling," my brother says. "I read the paper too and all I have to say is forget about it. What happened no longer matters."

"Yes, it does," I answer. "You told me you put her on the bus to Charlotte."

"Listen, Eugene, we're *not* talking about this, with each other or with anyone else, ever."

"You and I are, and now."

"If you've got enough brain cells left to understand that I know what's best, never," Bill says, with a harshness I've heard directed at me only once before.

"We're talking about this."

"Are you hearing me?" my brother says. "Just being on the phone is . . . Listen to me, hang up and keep your mouth shut and never mention her to me or anyone else, *ever.*"

"I'm not doing that," I answer.

For a few moments there is only silence.

"Okay, Eugene," Bill sighs, "but not on the phone, in person."

"Where?"

"My office."

"When?"

"Tomorrow morning. I've got surgery at eight, but I can meet you at eleven, unless I'm needed in the ER."

"I don't want to wait that long."

"Well, you have to, and don't call again, or e-mail, or talk to *anyone* about this, even if they bring it up. Just be here at eleven, and you damn well better be sober."

I hang up and pour another shot of whiskey in my glass tumbler. Night drifts into the neighborhood, veiling first the street and sidewalk, then my neighbor's yard and house. The streetlight comes on, hesitates, flickers. So too memory: A summer night when Sarah was three, carrying her out of the house and onto the porch steps. *Goodnight, moon,* we both said, and Sarah, pointing at the fireflies, *More moons, more moons.* It was something I'd have written in a notebook a year or two earlier, but by then my weekends and evenings spent writing had ceased. I'd rationalize it wasn't the drinking that kept me from writing; it was my choosing to be more to Kay and Sarah than a clacking typewriter behind a closed door. But that was just another lie.

I check the kitchen clock again. As I refill the tumbler with ice and whiskey, I try to calculate the hours until I can talk to my brother, but I keep losing count. Besides, don't I already know who was responsible for what happened to Ligeia Mosely? I'd been at Panther Creek when the threat was made. I was the one who'd brought her there in the first place.

CHAPTER FOUR

I n San Francisco, the Summer of Love occurred in 1967, but it took two years to arrive in small-town Appalachia. There had been a sighting on the interstate of a hippie driving a multicolored minibus in February, duly reported in the *Sylva Herald,* but otherwise the counterculture had been something strange seen on TV, exotic as a penguin or kangaroo tree. That June the only hints of change were a couple of UNC students who'd returned from Chapel Hill with shaggier hair. Our grandfather didn't allow our hair to touch our collars, but Bill wouldn't have worn his long anyway.

On the Tuesday after we'd met Ligeia, Grandfather sent us on our weekly rounds to deliver messages to patients who didn't have phones. They tended to live out in the country so we often passed the town's swimming pool on the way. Bill slowed to look at the girls sunning themselves.

"I thought Ligeia might be out there."

"She doesn't look like she lies out in the sun much."

"That's true," Bill said. "You'd think every girl from Florida would have a serious tan."

"Maybe she just doesn't mind being different," I said. "That's not such a bad thing."

We finished our errands but as we drove back, Bill turned right instead of going straight into town.

"I thought we'd see if Ligeia does live up here," he said. "If she's outside, we can ask her to sneak out a little of her parents' whiskey."

We crossed Panther Creek Bridge, then turned left onto Chestnut Road. We passed a few nice two-story farmhouses in the bottomland but as the road wound upward, trailers and weatherworn houses appeared, often with rusty car husks and broken appliances in the side yards. Some of these people were on welfare. We never delivered messages to them, and even when they made appointments themselves, Grandfather demanded Shirley send paying patients back to the treatment rooms first. On some days, he refused to see welfare patients at all.

"Her parents would want a good view," Bill said as we passed another shabby house and yard, "so they're probably up top."

The road curved and we passed another small A-frame, MOSELY neatly painted on the mailbox. The grass was cut and the house newly painted, but the lot was small, with nothing to look out at except trees that blocked any long view. A classmate of mine, Bennie Mosely, lived here. His dad worked on the county's DOT crew, as did Bennie during the summer. Mr. Mosely was a lay preacher as well. In middle school, Bennie and I hung out together at recess. Hopeless athletes both, we were always among the unchosen, so we sat on bench ends waiting for the bell to ring. We'd even spent a few nights at each other's houses.

The road continued another quarter mile, but no more homes appeared. This land had been recently clear-cut, the stumps like stones in a country grave-yard. The road curved a last time and there were only woods in front of us.

"Maybe she didn't leave until after we had," I said as Bill turned the truck around.

Then, as we passed the Moselys' house again, Bill slowed. A green bathing suit hung over a clothesline. No one was outside, and though Bill slowed even more, no one came to the door or window.

"So that's Ligeia's vacation home," Bill said as he sped back up. "Did you catch the name on the mail-box?"

"Mosely," I answered. "I go to school with Bennie Mosely. He lives there."

"So Ligeia's his sister?"

"Bennie's sister is your age. Her name is Tanya."

"I remember Tanya," Bill said. "She dropped out our senior year, which surprised me, because she was a good student. Maybe she got in 'trouble.' You know what that means?"

"Yes, Bill, I know what it means," I answered. "It means anyone who's pregnant."

"Not anyone, little brother. It's almost always a female."

"That's real funny," I muttered, and turned to look out the passenger window.

"Anyway, the last time I saw Tanya she was working at Hardee's. Do you know if she still works there?"

"How should I know?" I asked, still looking out the window. "I don't know much about anything, right?"

"Quit being so damn sensitive, Eugene," Bill said, "just because Mom . . ."

"Just because Mom thinks I'm what?" I asked when Bill paused.

"Nothing," Bill answered, more softly. "Look, I was just kidding around, okay? This weekend the beer's on me."

We were on the four-lane before either of us spoke again.

"Tanya's still working at Hardee's," I said. "She's the manager."

"We need to stop by there then," Bill said. "I'm wondering if Ligeia's just pretending to be from Florida."

"What are you going to say to Tanya?"

"I'll ask about a couple of classmates," Bill answered, "then work around to saying I saw someone in her yard I didn't recognize."

I waited in the truck while Bill went inside. When he came back out, the look on his face appeared caught between grin and grimace.

"What did she tell you?" I asked when he got in.

"A lot," Bill said, "a whole lot."

At six o'clock I watch the news on the Asheville station. Robbie Loudermilk, the county sheriff, asks anyone with information about Jane Mosely to contact his department. It had taken a week to identify her, he tells the reporter, and then only because dental records matched up with a 1969 missing person's report. No clothing or jewelry was among the remains, only shreds of a blue tarp. Loudermilk usually ambles about in an aw-shucks, Andy Griffith sort of way, but as I know very well, that can change into the tight-lipped anger I see now. He and Bill had played base-ball together, and been friends before my accident. There is no mention of leads or when Ligeia was last seen alive.

Another memory comes, not of the final time I saw Ligeia but a week before she disappeared, something mundane yet vivid. The mystery of memory. There's surely some scientific explanation for why the brain de-cides *Don't let go of this*. I've read novels and cannot recall a single character's name and yet I remember a red bicycle glanced once in a hardware-store window, a mole on a stranger's chin, a kitchen match lying beside a hearth. These remain, as does Ligeia reaching into her locker, a book crooked in her arm sliding free.

Of course, who can forget that first love, or first sex, or first drink—especially if they all occur together. I also remember how, after Ligeia had left our lives, I'd worried for months that she might reappear and tell Bill what I'd never confessed to him. But after a while nostalgia supplanted guilt and our summer at Panther Creek became more a tender coming-of-age story, a summer of love complete with bucolic setting.

Before today, when had I last thought of her? I have to think for a minute, then recall it was a month ago during a TV segment about South Beach. A woman with long red hair mixed a drink behind a posh bar. Younger than Ligeia would be, but it had brought her to mind. I'd wondered if she'd ended up like me or settled into a good life, perhaps with a husband and children. When the television show switched to a crowded boulevard, I'd studied the passersby for a glimpse of her, unlikely as it was.

Despite the whiskey, cold spreads from my chest to my fingertips, because now I never need imagine or search for her again. Any surmise was answered when a bank on Panther Creek crumbled after a hard rain, exposing blue tarp and bone amid the mud. I finish my last drink and walk upstairs to the bathroom I'd once shared with Bill. My bathroom now, my house, because after the divorce and my being fired from the community college, I'd come to live here with my mother, who'd been diagnosed with leukemia. *It's your house now, Eugene. I've already got the deed transferred to your name,* Bill had told me after our mother's funeral. *You deserve it for looking after her these last two years.*

But that was not true. Bill and Leslie had done as much, visiting every weekend, setting up appointments and paying for the various doctors, the medicine, everything else that ensured our mother's last days were as comfortable as possible. Bill's tenderness toward our mother, how he sat with her for hours, how he prayed with her, reaffirmed how much he'd changed because of Leslie. He was an exemplary husband and father, and a wonderful uncle to Sarah, never forgetting a birthday, helping her find summer jobs. He'd paid for her braces and later her college when Sarah refused the money I'd offered. As my daughter had told me numerous times, Bill was more of a father to her than I had been.

My mother agreed that Leslie's effect on Bill had been all for the good, but she also believed Bill became a better person because our grandfather's influence on him ended with Bill and Leslie's engagement. Despite what our mother and father had done, or perhaps because of it, one of our grandfather's stipulations was that my brother and I couldn't marry until our schooling was complete. Grandfather had been true to his word. When Bill entered Bowman Gray, he'd paid his own way with student loans and what Leslie made as a lab technician. As far as I know, Bill and Grandfather never spoke after he'd told the old man, face-to-face in his office, of the engagement. Grandfather hadn't attended the wedding and Bill had not attended our grandfather's funeral. *The only reason I'd have gone would have been to throw dirt on the son of a bitch,* Bill had told me, the bitterest comment I've ever heard him make.

Their estrangement was to my benefit. When Grandfather's will was read, my mother received the house she lived in and also half his savings. The rest, including the money from the sale of his office, house, and land, went to me. Bill's sole bequest was the Rembrandt print now hanging on his office wall. I'd offered to give Bill half but he refused. So I was left with enough money to buy all the wine and whiskey I'd ever desire.

CHAPTER FIVE

The mystery of your mermaid has been solved," Bill said as we pulled out of the Hardee's parking lot. "She is from Daytona Beach but staying with the Moselys for the summer. She's seventeen years old and Mr. Mosely's niece. According to Tanya, Ligeia's been giving her parents all sorts of grief. She ran off to a commune last summer and it took them a month to find her. Tanya says the parents want to get Ligeia away from 'bad influences.' They don't even allow her to be in town except for church."

Then it was Saturday and we'd finished waxing and buffing our grandfather's office. As we cooled off next to the air conditioner, Bill leaned forward, head down, nodding slightly as he deliberated. I thought how rare it was for him to be indecisive.

"Maybe we shouldn't go out there tomorrow," he said, more to himself than to me.

"I don't think she's a bad person," I said.

"I didn't say she was, Eugene, but what Tanya said . . ."

"You think we should be scared to be around her?"

"I'm not saying that," Bill answered.

"I'm not scared of her," I said. "Besides, I checked in the closet Wednesday when you were with Grandfather," I added. "There are plenty of Valium and Quaalude samples."

"You shouldn't have done that," Bill said tersely.

But you can, I almost answered. Bill leaned forward again, and then nodded as he took a deep breath.

"Okay," he said, and left me in the front room to watch for Nebo.

When he returned, his open palm revealed a packet containing two white pills.

"Prescription filled," he said. "But we're not going to be stupid, little brother. This prescription has no refills."

The next day we loaded the fishing gear but didn't drive straight to the stream. Bill stopped at the convenience store outside town and came out with a brown paper bag, in it a six-pack of Michelob and a bottle of Strawberry Hill.

"Try not to let those beers shake much," he said, handing me the sack. "Of course with all that Aqua Velva you splashed on your face, my Aqua Velva, I might add, you could probably get drunk just licking around your lips. Anyway, it's aftershave, not cologne, Eugene. If you want to smell good for a girl, use British Sterling or Jade East."

A car pulled up beside us and Bill motioned for me to put the bag on the floorboard. Renee Brock, whose father owned the jewelry store, got out of the car and went inside.

"Let's get out of here," Bill said, backing up the truck. We turned onto the four-lane and headed toward Panther Creek.

Something could happen today that I will never forget, I told myself. *Or it won't happen.* I was thinking that too, because I could simply walk upstream and fish, leaving Bill at the pool. My heart quickened as we turned onto the gravel road and then the logging trail. We parked and walked through the mountain laurel to the stream.

"Looks like we got here first," Bill said as lifted the wine and six-pack from the grocery bag. "Put them in the stream, but not where they'll wash away."

I set the cans and bottle in the water. A trout leaped in the pool's center and a ring rippled outward, giving me a bull's-eye for a cast. When I turned to get a rod and reel, Bill's face was perplexed.

"What's wrong?"

"Nothing," he said. "Like they say, if it feels good, do it, right? And with Leslie way up in Virginia. I know we've been dating awhile but it's not like we're engaged." Bill paused. "Anyway, Ligeia probably won't show up. Even if she does, she might decide you're more her type. Isn't that what hippies are into, feelings and expressing yourself? According to Mom, that's you, not me, right?"

When I didn't respond, Bill took a thin foil packet from his front pocket and handed it to me.

"So here," Bill said. "You know what it is, don't you?"

"Of course."

"You know how to put one on?"

"Sure," I said, though not so sure.

"Make certain you *do* put it on, little brother. Even if hippies believe in free love, that doesn't mean they can't get pregnant. They can get other things as well."

"I know that. I'm not a kid anymore, in case you haven't noticed," I said, taking the condom. "What about you?"

Bill patted the front pocket of his jeans. I put mine in my pocket too as he walked over to the stream and pulled two beers free from the plastic ring, tossing one to me.

"Since, as you say, you're not a kid anymore."

I held the can but made no move to pull the metal tab.

"That's all right," I said, holding the beer out to him.

"I figured you were lying about not ever drinking," my brother said, "but damn, not even once?"

"No."

"Go ahead and pull the tab," Bill said. "It's not a hand grenade."

The tone in his voice, part instructive, part exasperation, was one I'd heard too often. *When a curveball's thrown, don't rock back on your heels,* he'd chided me when I tried out for Little League. But I had always rocked back. *That's okay,* he'd told me after I failed to make the team. *It's just not who you are.* He'd said it with a pat on the back, maybe even meaning well, but it rankled then and did so now. On such a hot summer day, the can's chilled dampness felt good on my palm and fingers. Surely its cold contents would feel even better sliding down my throat.

I pulled the tab, a soft sucking sound as the tin separated. Foam rose and covered the top. I wiped it off and raised the can and swallowed. It didn't taste good, but I knew instantly I could get used to that bitterness. That I *would* get used to it. I looked through the trees toward the road and felt a spasm of panic. Here I was, underage and drinking, out in the open, and on a Sunday, and with a condom in my pocket. I drank quickly, hoping to blot out the sense of being observed from the heavens and by a grandfather who seemed as omnipresent as God. I tossed my empty on the bank, belched loudly, then went to the creek and pulled free another can. As I opened it and took a long swallow, I didn't experience what I'd read later in *Cat on a Hot Tin Roof,* the "click" Brick spoke of. No, what I felt on this Sunday afternoon was a gliding sensation, then a soft smooth landing where the world greeted me with a warm glowing smile.

"Damn, little brother," Bill said, still holding his first beer. "It's not a contest."

"I don't think she's coming," I said a few minutes later.

"Doesn't appear so," Bill agreed.

But when we looked downstream, Ligeia was coming down the opposite bank. She paused on the rock slab and took off her flip-flops and a T-shirt with JEFFERSON AIRPLANE printed on the front. She swam across and walked toward us, the water streaming off her. The alcohol allowed me to settle my eyes fully on her. She was prettier than she'd seemed before and everything about her was more vivid—the varied hues of her love beads, the green bathing suit, the fingernails trimmed to narrow *V*'s. Most of all the depths of her blue eyes. I took another swallow of my third beer while Bill nursed his second.

"So where's the happening?" Ligeia asked.

"Right here," Bill answered, handing her the Valium.

"Just two?"

"And this," Bill said, lifting the wine bottle from the stream. He screwed off the cap. "Strawberry Hill, as ordered."

"Have you got a glass or cup?" she asked.

"We forgot to pack wineglasses," Bill said. "From what your cousin Tanya says, it wouldn't bother you any more than it bothers us."

Her eyes hardened.

"So the word's out that Preacher Mosely is trying to save his wayward niece," she said. "What did Tanya say about me?"

"Not much," Bill said. "That you live in Daytona Beach but your parents thought you needed to be away from some bad influences down there. And that you're seventeen; she told me that too."

For a few moments, Ligeia didn't speak. Then the right side of her cheek flexed into a wry smile.

"Looks like the bad influences part hasn't worked out," she said, taking the bottle. "Haven't you at least got a paper cup?"

"I've got a used one," Bill answered. "I can wash it out in the creek for you."

"Do that," she said.

Bill disappeared into the mountain laurel.

"So you'll be what, a junior this year?" she asked, and I nodded.

"Do you know Bennie?"

"Yes," I said, talking slow to keep my words from slurring. "We're in the same glade."

"Same *glade*, like in the Everglades," Ligeia said, and grinned. "It sounds like you've got a head start on me."

"I guess so," I said, grinning too. "You'll be a senior?"

"Not for long. As soon as I turn eighteen I'm out of Daytona and headed to Miami."

"Tanya said you were in a hippie commune. Is that true?"

"I was there a month," Ligeia answered, "then the cops came and took me back to Daytona."

"Is the commune near Miami?"

"It's twenty miles from there."

"But you'll be here until you turn eighteen?"

"God, I hope not," Ligeia said. "Do you know them, my aunt and uncle?"

"Yes," I answered. "I've spent the night at Bennie's a few times."

"Then you know they'd wig out if they knew what I'm doing right now. For them, everything from smoking cigarettes to saying 'damn' is a sin. And the only thing they play on their radio is Jesus music. They even get bent if I don't wear a bra."

"They're strict, I guess, but they always seemed nice."

"I guess they're nice enough, Bennie too," Ligeia said. "A hell of a lot nicer than my mom and old man, but, damn, every five minutes they're praying or reading the Bible. It's Jesus this or Jesus that morning to night. It is so nowhere. Even Jesus freaks need to mellow out once in a while. And their idea of fun is going to the Dairy Queen. There and church are the only places they've taken me since I got up here. I started coming down here just to get away from it for a while."

Bill came back. He went to the creek and washed out the cup, filled it with wine, and handed it to her.

"You guys aren't into these?" she asked, showing the pills before she swallowed them.

Bill shook his head.

"How about pot?"

"We like a straight beer buzz," Bill said. "Right, Eugene?"

"Damn straight," I said and grinned.

I finished the beer with a long swallow and leaned to set the can down. As I did I lost my balance and fell to the ground. Bill helped me to my feet.

"I think you've drunk enough, little brother," he said, and turned to Ligeia. "His first time."

"No shit," Ligeia said.

"She really was in a commune," I told Bill, and when he didn't say anything I asked her what it was like.

"Plenty of drugs and music, nobody telling you what to do, that was the best part. If it feels good, you just do it. And you shared everything, and I mean everything. There was this abandoned farmhouse we all crashed in, and the ocean was only half a mile away so you could go there any time. One of the guys had lived in San Francisco and he'd rigged this far-out speaker system in the trees. That was so cool, because it was like the trees were making the music, and all day and all night. Quicksilver, the Dead, Jefferson Airplane."

I nodded at the shirt on the rock slab.

"That's a music group?"

"You haven't heard of them?"

I shook my head.

"How about the Grateful Dead, or Quicksilver, or Moby Grape?"

"No," I said.

"Jesus Christ," Ligeia said. "This place is like going back in time. All I've heard on the radio is hillbilly music and preachers."

"There are a couple of top-forty stations," I said.

"They won't be playing these groups, though," she said. "Maybe at night something hip might come on. Of course, Uncle Hiram and Aunt Cazzie won't be listening to it."

A rod tip quivered and I reeled in a foot-long rainbow trout. After a couple of ham-fisted attempts, I pinned it to the sand, the fish throbbing against my palm. I freed the hook, gilled the trout onto the stringer, and placed it in the shallows.

"Do you eat them?" Ligeia asked after a swallow of wine.

"Our grandfather does," Bill said. "Our mother cooks them for him."

"The grandfather who's the doctor?"

"Yes."

I rebaited the hook and cast but I missed the water and snagged a rhododendron limb on the far bank.

"Oops," I said, and laughed.

I jerked the hook free and recast, missing where I aimed but at least hitting water. For a few minutes I watched the rods as Ligeia and Bill stood behind me. Then Ligeia gave a soft *umm*.

"Damn, I've missed having a buzz," she said. "Uncle Hiram told me he drank alcohol only once. He said he liked being loaded so much he never drank again. I thought that was the point, to feel good."

"Hell yeah, to feel good," I echoed.

"So how are you feeling?" Ligeia asked my brother.

"Very good," Bill answered, and set his can by the tackle box.

"Me too," she said, her voice as dreamy as her eyes, "though being a mermaid I'd feel even groovier in the water. How about you? Feel like getting wet with me, Bill?"

For a moment my brother didn't say anything.

"Well," he said, "it might scare the fish away."

Ligeia smiled.

"I don't mean here," she said, picking up the wine bottle, "downstream."

"Yeah," Bill said, blushing slightly. "I guess that's better. If we swim there, we won't scare the fish."

"That's right," she said. "We don't want to scare the fish."

When they got to the downstream pool, Ligeia refilled her cup and, drink in hand, she waded into the water. I freshened the bait on the second rod and made another sloppy cast. Soon the rod tip dipped. I reeled in a nice rainbow and raised it for Bill to see. But he wasn't looking my way. He and Ligeia were closer now, not an arm's length apart. I placed the trout on the stringer and dropped it back in the water. When I looked downstream again, the plastic cup was drifting into the tailrace. Bill and Ligeia were up to their waists in water, face-to-face as Ligeia reached behind her and the green bikini top fell free.

CHAPTER SIX

Cases like this can be difficult to solve, but we've received more forensic information, and some input from the comunity. We've also been reviewing the original missing person's report from 1969. Unfortunately, the uncle and aunt who filed the report are deceased, as are the victim's parents. The burial site's proximity to the interstate is being considered. We know of at least one serial killer in the region at that time. Of course, we ask anyone with information to contact the sheriff's department."

These are Robbie Loudermilk's words in the next morning's paper. The story has been relegated to page two, but near the article's end the reporter asks if Loudermilk knows of other cases in Jackson County where human remains had been found. One, he answers, almost certainly a suicide, had been identified in 1962. Then Loudermilk mentions a case in 1921 that I already know about. "Not a whole skeleton but a femur," the sheriff notes, "found by a dog on the banks of the Tuckaseegee." A cloud covering the sun on an otherwise clear day—something of that same darkening chill passes over me as I link what was found in 1921 to Ligeia.

I can no longer simply sit and wait, so get in my car and drive out of Sylva and then north on I-40 until I come to the second Asheville exit. The medical center rises into view. I haven't been here in fifteen years, and then not to Bill's office but to the hospital recovery room where my daughter lay.

Three events, each decades apart, merge. Coincidence, or something more—blood connected by blood.

I'm early so expect to be flipping through magazines until Bill arrives, but the receptionist takes me straight to his office.

"Dr. Matney said he'd be here within the hour."

I sit in the leather armchair opposite Bill's desk. Despite the personal touches, the office has an antiseptic feel, as if minutes earlier each item was lifted and sterilized, then reset exactly where it had been. A laptop's on the huge oak desk, as well as photographs of Leslie and my nephews, Lee and Jesse, and a photograph of

Sarah at her college graduation. Bill's AOA certificate and Bowman Gray degree hang on the wall beside the desk. Below are two photographs of Bill. One is of him in his high school baseball uniform. In the other my brother is outside a tent in Haiti with two Red Cross workers. He's in a stained blue smock and clearly exhausted but smiling, as are the Red Cross workers.

Behind me, though, and much less cheerful, is the print of Rembrandt's *The Anatomy Lesson of Dr. Nicolaes Tulp*, which once hung in our grandfather's examination room. Considering their antipathy, I'd been surprised when Bill accepted this inheritance. It's hung where most patients won't notice it and that seems wise. To see a man performing an autopsy would be unsettling for someone anticipating surgery. The weighty mahogany frame makes the scene darker, more ominous. "That painting is a reminder," Bill had answered when I'd asked why it hung in his office, "of why I can never be complacent."

On the bookshelf, thick tomes of the trade. No novels or biographies, but on the row beside Menezes and Sonntag's *Principles of Spinal Surgery* and Kaye and Black's *Operative Neurosurgery* is the copy of my M.A. thesis on Thomas Wolfe, which I gave Bill thirty-six years ago. *It's a wonderful piece of scholarship, Eugene,* Bill said after he'd read it. *You perceive so much, things I wouldn't have noticed.* I'd had the disorienting sense that my brother was truly proud of me, even a bit envious. My thesis appears thin and insubstantial amid the medical books, but it is still here, as is, I now notice on the shelf, our mother's Bible.

My thesis, our mother's Bible, the painting—all bespeak a humility so unlike the brother I'd grown up with who was so certain of what was best for him and me. It was easy for Bill to see himself as above the rest of us. In school the smartest student, on the field the best athlete, handsome and popular, and, all the while, Grandfather assuring him and everyone else in Sylva that Bill would become a great surgeon. Who would dare argue against our grandfather's decree? How could Bill even imagine himself as anything but the golden boy?

When Bill married Leslie, I was skeptical that this new version of my brother would last. So many people, seemingly transformed by spouses, revert to their old ways. Your mate believes you're better than you are, and for a while you actually believe it too. But a day comes when you don't believe it anymore and soon your spouse doesn't either, and you might remind her of where she'd met you in the first place, and the tumbler of whiskey that lay on the bar between her and you, and she'll say, Yes, I met you in a bar. I just didn't know you'd live your life as though you'd never left it.

But by all appearances Bill remained transformed. A good man, compassionate, generous, helping with all manner of good causes. I'd seen articles noting such in the Asheville newspaper, seen my brother interviewed on WLOS for some charity or cause. Bill was disappointed when I'd left the Ph.D. program and settled for teaching at a community college, disappointed once more when I'd stopped writing fiction. But he had kept encouraging me, urging me to use my "gift."

After the drinking got out of control, he came to see me, brandishing the thesis. *You have a rare abiltiy for writing and understanding literature, Eugene,* he told me. *If you get your head right, you can turn things around. You can teach at a university; you can write books.* I'd responded with a drunken tirade. He finally left, but not before nodding at the bedroom's shut door where Kay had taken Sarah. *Life's a gift, Eugene,* he'd said. *Don't squander it.*

After the wreck, Bill hired the best trial lawyer in western North Carolina to defend me, but the anger once directed at Grandfather now was directed at me. *You have no idea what you've been given and now thrown away, but damn it, I'll not let you waste another person's life.* Two days later Kay and Sarah left to stay with Bill's family. They remained there until Bill found them an apartment in Asheville. *Your brother's as fine a man as I know.* How many times had I heard that over the years, and with it the sometimes subtle, sometimes more direct, indictment of me? Always the better brother. But now everything seemed helter-skelter.

I waited for a man who'd lied to me for forty-six years. Something terrible had happened to Ligeia at Panther Creek and my brother had done it, but how to believe Bill capable of such a thing, toward anyone. *Murder.* An ambulance wails in the distance but is coming closer, as if bringing that word toward me, increasingly louder, shriller. The ambulance turns into the hospital entrance and red light washes over Bill's window. The siren dies and a memory of a high school baseball game fills the silence. Bill had hit a deep ball to right field and decided to stretch a triple into a home run. The catcher took the throw at the plate, too late for a tag, but as Bill slid, he stabbed his metal cleats into Bill's knee, a cheap shot that could have ended my brother's baseball career. Bill got to his feet and picked up the bat, gripping it like a club. The catcher stepped back, and kept backing up as my brother limped after him until teammates wrestled Bill into the dugout. Would Bill have swung that bat? And if so, at a knee or a rib cage or the catcher's head? All I know is that the rage made anything seem possible.

I hear my brother speaking to his receptionist. In a few moments he comes in, closes the door, and sits down in his desk chair. His hair is thinning and a few more crow's-feet crease his eyes, but his regimen of exercise, eating well, and moderate drinking makes him appear a decade younger. He looks at me as he might a patient about to receive an unwelcome diagnosis.

"Believe me, Eugene," he says softly. "You're better off not knowing about this, better off in a lot of ways."

"And why is that?"

"It didn't involve you then," Bill says, "and it doesn't now."

"It did, and it does."

"Just let me—"

"Tell me what happened, damn it."

"Listen to me," he says, less gently. "Think about the decisions you've made in your life and how they've turned out. Let me make this one for you. Trust me enough to do that."

"Trust?" I answer. "You told me you took Ligeia to the bus station. You told me you *saw her leave.*"

"I lied for your own good."

"Tell me what happened. I'm not leaving until you do."

Bill raises a hand to his brow, holds it there briefly as if confirming a fever. He sets the hand on the armrest.

"Okay," he says.

"When I went to meet her that morning, I didn't see her, not at first. But then I started looking around and saw a red suitcase in the creek. Ligeia was lying on a sandbar downstream. I didn't get a pulse but I did CPR. I did it a long time. There was blood and a bump on the back of her head. She probably slipped and hit her head on a rock. Carrying that suitcase could have caused her to lose her balance, but she might have been drugged up too. That could have caused her to slip."

"She lost consciousness and drowned?"

"Yes."

I try to hold enough thoughts together to comprehend what I'm hearing, but it's like passing a hand through cobwebs. It sounds impossible, but what would be more possible, that Bill had killed her?

"Why didn't you take her to the hospital, or go to a house and call the rescue squad?"

"It wouldn't have done any good."

"It wouldn't have done any good?"

"My doing CPR was her only chance," Bill says. "Maybe if I'd seen the suitcase sooner, or gotten to the creek earlier . . ."

"I'm not talking about that. You know what I mean."

"I panicked, Eugene. If I called, even from a pay phone, they'd figure out who called it in. You probably won't remember but it rained the night before. Tire prints and footprints would be there."

"But if it was just an accident?"

"But I was there," Bill says, "and she had a suitcase with her."

"So?"

"Damn it," Bill says, annoyance in his voice now. "She had a suitcase. Someone was clearly going to meet her, and I was the one who showed up. There would have been questions, and with her getting in all that trouble in Florida, questions about drugs, questions about a lot of things." Bill pauses. "There would have been an autopsy, and even though it was an accident, it would still look suspicious . . ."

"So you buried her?"

"Yes."

Then I understood.

"You were afraid it would keep you out of med school?"

Bill is silent.

"That's it, isn't it?" I ask, a long-absent self-righteousness in my tone. "Med school was more important than Ligeia's family knowing what had happened, more important than her being buried out there like a damn dog?"

"Judge me if you want," Bill says, "but if you had been in the same situation . . ."

"I've fucked up my life, I admit that. I've done some bad things, but I have never done anything close to this."

"Haven't you?" Bill says, looking at me meaningfully.

"If you mean the car accident," I answer, "that's what it was, an *accident*."

"And this was an accident too, and when you had yours, you acted no differently. You could have turned down the attorney I got you and gone to jail."

"You covered her up with dirt and left her. Except for someone being out there right after a hard rain, no one may have ever known."

I meet my brother's eyes. They are gray but with a yellow tinge, like butternut. Our mother's eyes were the same color, another small detail our grandfather could not control.

"No one knew, that is, except you."

"And if I hadn't done what I did," Bill says, and gestures toward the door, "I wouldn't be here helping people, and Ligeia would be just as dead, whether in the woods or a cemetery."

"So it all turned out for the best?"

"I'm not saying that," Bill replies. "All I'm saying is that some—no, a lot of good has happened because I did leave her out there."

Bill's landline flashes but he checks the number and doesn't pick up.

"You should have told me the truth when you came home that night," I tell him. "I asked you if everything was okay. You said it was."

"You couldn't have changed anything, it was already done," Bill answers. "I made a decision and it was for the best, then and now."

"Best for you, Bill, not me."

"How would your life have been better? For forty-six years you'd have known she was out there dead."

"Ligeia wouldn't have been out there forty-six years," I answer. "She wouldn't have been out there a day."

"You can't know that, Eugene. If you had been there . . ."

"All these years and you've never told anyone?"

Bill shakes his head.

"Not even Leslie?"

"What don't you understand about this?" my brother says, opening his palms in exasperation. "What good would come of that for Leslie, in any possible way?"

"So it's just something to know and then forget about?" I ask. "You never lie awake, thinking about her being out there? You've never wanted to tell someone, get it off your chest?"

"That's not your concern," he answers tersely.

"But it's not your secret anymore, and with her being buried, they'll believe she was murdered. Ligeia knew people. She could have told them about us."

"None of her friends said anything about us when she disappeared."

"Everyone thought she'd run off to Miami. Now they'll know different."

"No one ever saw us out there with her," Bill answers, "not once."

I've sunk deeper into the chair's soft upholstery. I push against the arms, reposition myself closer to the edge. Go ahead and say it, I tell myself, and do.

"What if they find out she wasn't in that grave alone, Bill?"

"It's not possible," Bill says, rising from his chair again. "Now you know what happened. Keep quiet about it and in a few days this will be out of the papers."

"So just go on with my life, like nothing's happened."

"That shouldn't be hard, Eugene," my brother says, "since your life involves little more than opening a bottle."

When I don't respond, Bill picks up an ink pen and taps the desk twice, as if testing the wood's solidity.

"Some people die sooner than others, Eugene, including our father. You know what Grandfather said to me when I declared premed at Wake Forest? He said, *'Bill, my boy, once you get your degree you'll know that, had you been at the hospital that day instead of some butcher, you could have saved your own father's life.'* It was a screwed-up thing for that old bastard to say, but it haunts me. I've even dreamed I did the operation and saved Dad."

Bill pauses but I have no response.

"You don't remember him, our father I mean?"

"Not really."

"He was a good dad," Bill says. "I remember this thing he did with me. I liked the smell of his aftershave and once he put his on he'd splash some on my cheeks too. It was a little thing, but he never forgot to do it every morning, even if he was running late."

"And you're suddenly telling me these things why?" I ask.

"I think about what Grandfather told me, how if I'd been the one operating I could have saved our father."

"What in the hell are you trying to say?"

"I'm just trying to put what happened in some context."

"Context," I say. "That's a nice abstract term."

"You've always been better with words than me," Bill says. "Use whatever ones you want, but here's the thing. Whatever you say or do won't help Ligeia. It won't help her family. Her parents and younger sister are all dead, her uncle and aunt are dead. But think about who else you'll hurt, even if you don't give a damn about me. Leslie, your nephews. And Sarah, her too. And I'm also saying that, brief as it was, I feel I *had* a father, I knew him, and you never had that so, yes, at times I've tried to be more than just a big brother. I've done things the way I thought best for you as well as for me. This is one of them."

Bill looks at his watch, then nods at the photograph of himself in Haiti.

"I'm going back in September. What I can do is help the living, and that's what I need to do now. I've got an operation I need to prep for. Are we clear about all of this?"

"All of it?" I answer. "No."

"But enough to keep your mouth shut about it?"

After a few moments I nod.

"Good," he says.

"Sarah," I ask. "She still keeps in touch with you. Doesn't she?"

"Yes."

"She's doing well?"

"Yes."

"Can you give me her phone number, or e-mail? I could go to the library and use a computer."

"You know she's asked me not to do that."

"Could I at least see a photograph?"

"I need to go," Bill says, but when I ask again, he leans over his computer. After a few clicks, my brother turns the screen so I can see.

I almost don't recognize this young woman, professionally dressed, hair cut short. Then I look at the face more closely, see the slightly snubbed nose she got from her mother, the gray eyes from me, and, of course, the crescent shape above her left brow.

"She's a beautiful young woman," my brother says.

"Yes," I answer, because she is.

He clicks to another photograph, this one less formal. Though she is inside, she wears a heavy wool overcoat. Bill clicks and the photograph is replaced by an e-mail. *Dear Uncle Bill, Wanted you to see the coat I bought with the birthday money. Thanks sooo much. Love, Sarah.*

"Just her mailing address, Bill," I ask as he logs off. "She can't mind that."

He shakes his head.

"Just that," I say, my voice softening almost to a whisper.

"Give her time, Eugene," Bill says. "Try to see it from her point of view. Do you know what Sarah remembers most about her weekends growing up? It's the clinking of ice cubes falling into a glass tumbler. She says the sooner it began, the worse the day would be."

CHAPTER SEVEN

I drive down I-40 to the Sylva exit but instead of my usual route home I go straight into town. Little has changed since my childhood. Businesses have different owners and different names, and another stoplight has been added, but the buildings themselves are the same. Main Street ends in front of the same grassy hill, atop it the white marble courthouse that looms over the town, the same huge clock on the facade. At night the hill darkens except for the clock face, which brightens the sky like a second moon.

The road makes a *t*. I turn left onto Randolph Lane, park across from the square redbrick building. The shrubbery has been dug up but otherwise the yard is much the same. Above the awning is the metal shingle that Nebo repainted every spring, retracing the black words WILLIAM MATNEY M.D., then painting the rest white. BLUE RIDGE BOUTIQUE the sign says now.

In an interview I once read, a surgeon at the Mayo Clinic said only those with an inherent degree of cruelty chose his profession. After Bill's sophomore year at Wake Forest, Grandfather let my brother do office procedures, ones where glistening steel sutured flesh. *When a surgeon creates a wound, he needs to know how to close it,* he'd told Bill, so as Grandfather watched, Bill stitched flesh ripped open by glass and metal. But there were also opportunities for a scalpel, even in a GP's office. Infections needed to be lanced, lesions removed.

"Watch how good he is with his hands," Grandfather bragged to the patients. "Have you ever seen better hand-eye coordination? That's why he's such a good ballplayer."

As I stare at my grandfather's former office, it's easy to believe the Mayo surgeon was right, and that the supposed breach between Grandfather and Bill was not so great after all. An inherited cruelty. The acrid, sterile smells; the bleak white walls and cold linoleum floors; the trays of glistening metal instruments—all had enhanced a sense of detachment from other people's suffering. But that had not been enough for my grandfather. A single framed print hung in each examination room. One was of Leonardo's anatomical sketch of a disembodied human hand, in the other room the Rembrandt now in Bill's office. As a child I'd found those pictures, as I did Nebo, the source of nightmares. I did not enter the rooms unless coerced. Yet Bill had been drawn here, and when offered the chance to cut and stitch and probe he'd not hesitated. *The painting is a reminder of why I can never be complacent,* Bill had said about the Rembrandt, but now I wonder if his displaying the print was more an act of nostalgia.

No one in Sylva complained, at least openly, about Bill's involvement, which spoke of Bill's competence but also the respect, and fear, my grandfather had garnered from being the town's sole doctor for four decades. If patients didn't finish an antibiotic or walked on a sprained ankle, Grandfather berated them, often in public, whether the person was a cashier at the drugstore or Mr. Ashbrook, who owned the bank. If it happened again, Grandfather refused to treat them, forcing a drive of twenty miles to Waynesville. *People make choices in life,* he'd told us often, *and you must accept the consequences of those choices.* He was on the town council, and there as elsewhere he was deferred to. At election time, local and state politicians vied for his support. In 1961, another doctor opened an office in Sylva, but after six months he had so few patients that he left. People were afraid not to keep going to Grandfather.

Because he knew all their secrets, my mother claimed. He knew which husband had contracted gonorrhea, which daughter needed to visit an aunt for a few months, which mother took Valium. After two, sometimes even three generations of his care, how could any family not have something potentially embarrassing? But now as I look at this boutique that was once my grandfather's office, I wonder if small-town doctors derive as much power in those moments they probe, with hands and eyes if not with instruments, the body's most intimate places. How many years afterward might a person, though fully dressed, yet feel that naked vulnerability, that sense of surrender, like a dog exposing its belly to another dog?

Those who hadn't known Grandfather might believe the war experience had made him the way he was. He had certainly suffered physical pain, as the truncated fingers proved, but trauma caused by fear seemed less likely. He'd told Bill and me that he never believed for an instant he would die in the war, even when the shrapnel tore into his fingers. *Some of us just knew we would live,* he'd said. *As long as we didn't tempt death, it would leave us alone.* Yet he had witnessed many others who suffered and died. Had it changed him? I'd asked my mother that question the day of his funeral.

"Your grandmother told me that when he was overseas, she'd prayed that he would not return," my mother had answered. "This was soon after your father and I married. Your grandmother wanted to prepare me, I suppose, for whatever he might say or do to me. I don't think he ever physically beat her, your father said not, but your grandmother always seemed to be waiting for that first slap or fist. I'd see it in her face and in her body, mostly in her eyes. I cannot remember a time when those eyes rose high enough to meet his, Eugene, not once. Her dying may have been the only thing she ever did without your grandfather's permission." But then my mother had paused. "Well, the *second* thing, which brings up the question of *when* during the war your grandmother started praying he'd not return. Funny, isn't it?" my mother had mused. "All these years and I've never thought of that before."

I have several photographs of my grandmother. One is when she is eighteen, at a cotillion, posing in the manner of a young woman well aware of her beauty. Then at age twenty-two in a *Sylva Herald* photograph at a war bond rally. She's dressed in a skirt and sweater but that same self-awareness is present, for the last time. Not the beauty, for my mother said she retained that into middle age, but the awareness that anyone would notice it, or that she would want them to.

During my early twenties when I thought that, like Wolfe, I might write my own small-town novel, I'd found a November 1918 article in the *Sylva Herald*'s archives. "Raleigh Peddler Arrested After Altercation with Sylva Doctor," the headline read. More articles had appeared in the following days. The evening after the confrontation, the salesman had disappeared. A fisherman mentioned seeing two men, one in a suit, another not well dressed and much taller, crossing the bridge outside town, but the following day the fisherman confessed to Sheriff Lunsford that he'd been drunk and seen no such thing, and Mr. Tillis, the hardware store owner, recalled the salesman had spoken of a desire to go to California. Although no one had seen him leave on the bus, the sheriff surmised that, like so many men in their twenties, the salesman had headed west with a thumb in the air and a sense of adventure. The salesman's family demanded a criminal inquiry, insisting that he would have contacted them as well as withdrawing his savings from the bank, but there wasn't one. Three years later a femur was found on the Tuckaseegee's banks. The family returned, having heard nothing from the missing man for three years. A more intense search of the woods surrounding the riverbank yielded nothing more.

I have several clear memories of my grandmother—her hunched body, her voice so soft, even to children, that she was hard to understand. What I remember most is her giving me a palmful of Luden's cough drops, the closest thing to candy in Grandfather's house. She'd died eight months after my father, lingering one day in the hospital after a heart attack. My mother had been with her. *She was lying in the bed and simply turned her back to me and the nurse. Your grandmother knew she was dying and was ready and who could blame her.*

Of course your grandfather never believed he would die, my mother had concluded. Bill had said the same thing about Grandfather, and so it had seemed prior to that evening in 1974 when I'd found him in this same brick building. It was during the Christmas holidays. I was home from Wake Forest when Nebo came to the house and motioned for me to go with him. He'd unlocked the office's back door and motioned me inside, but he did not follow. Grandfather's neck lay on the leather chair's headrest. He stared at the ceiling, eyes and mouth open. *Astonishment* seems so narratively predictable, but I know of no better word to describe the look on his face.

I'm startled, as if from sleep, when the door opens and a woman comes out with a blue-bowed gift. A boutique, not an office. I pull out of the parking space and turn left onto Church Street and in another block take another left. As I drive back through town, I try to recall all I can about the day and evening Ligeia disappeared. After school I had waited at home for Bill to return. Hours passed. I told myself that maybe he'd taken her to Asheville, or already come back and gone out again. When my mother asked where Bill was, I told her that I didn't know.

It was after dark when he came in. I was lying on the bed, the radio playing, the one station I left it on drifting in and out. Bill hadn't spoken to our mother, who was in the den, but had come up the stairs and straight to his bedroom. The door was locked but I pressed close and asked if everything was okay. Yes, he'd answered, Ligeia's on the bus to Charlotte. Just go to bed, he'd said. A few minutes later I heard the shower in the bathroom we shared. I may have listened to the radio a while longer or turned it off and closed my eyes, sleeping more easily than I had for days. I'm not sure. My next clear memory is of sitting at the breakfast table the next morning as my brother sat down to join me. A bruise purpled his left cheekbone and his upper lip was swollen.

"What on earth happened to your face?" our mother exclaimed.

"I was fishing," Bill answered. "A laurel branch whipped back and nailed me good."

I'd had branches do the same to me, and I knew he'd met Ligeia at Panther Creek. Surely that morning I'd have noticed if there were also scratch marks, the raking kind that fingernails make. Yet even so, why would I have thought Ligeia responsible? Or that she'd caused the bruise or swollen lip. After all, she'd boarded the bus to Charlotte and everything was fine. My brother had said so.

It is all so suddenly improbable—Ligeia falling in the water, hitting her head and drowning. A stream, a rock, a laurel branch. Improbable, but not impossible. To think otherwise, I have to believe my brother is a murderer.

PART TWO

CHAPTER EIGHT

D amn," Bill said that Sunday when he came back upstream. "You drank another beer?"

"Hell yeah, and look at this," I said, the words I spoke slippery as creek rocks. I lifted the stringer and showed Bill a fourteen-inch rainbow, the biggest we'd caught that summer.

"I guess it's your lucky day, and about to get better," Bill said, and nodded toward the woods downstream. "Ligeia's waiting for you."

"Why?" I asked.

"Why do you think?"

Years later I would read Faulkner's answer when someone asked why he drank. To feel braver and stronger, he'd answered, and I had been feeling exactly that way, but the sensation quickly drained away.

"Maybe it's not such a good idea. I've been thinking that if Grandfather found out . . ."

Bill shrugged, gave a slight smile.

"If you don't want to go, little brother, that's fine. I'm just the messenger."

"You don't think I will, do you?" I replied, meeting his eyes.

"I don't care either way," Bill said, no longer smiling. "But she's got to leave soon, so if you're going go now, though you might want to wash the worm and fish slime off your hands first."

I kneeled by the creek and rubbed my hands with sand and water. As I got up, the world seesawed a moment, then rebalanced.

"I'm going," I said.

Bill patted my jeans pocket.

"Don't forget to put that on," he said. "You understand?"

"Yeah, yeah," I mumbled.

Beer sloshed uneasily in my stomach, and the disconnect between my head and feet caused me to stumble twice. After that I kept my eyes on the ground as I made my way into the woods. Ligeia had her bikini on. She sat on the quilt, knees tucked. I stood above her, swaying slightly, unsure what to do or say.

"You can lay down beside me, Eugene," she said, giving me a drowsy smile. "I'm a wild child but I won't bite."

"If Bill asked you to . . ."

"He didn't ask me to do anything."

"I just don't want to be disrespectful," I said, slurring the last word.

Despite the Valium and wine, Ligeia's eyes hardened. I'd see that look again when I taught at the community college, always in the eyes of women who'd grown up hard, a distrust of anything spoken softly.

"*Respect*," Ligeia answered. "Is that what gets a girl's panties off up here?"

"I didn't mean, don't mean," I stammered. "It's just that Bill, he's better looking, and athletic."

Ligeia patted the quilt.

"Come sit with me, Eugene," she said, her voice softening.

I sat down on the quilt, flexed my knees and clasped my hands, mirroring her. My stomach calmed.

"You North Carolina boys," she sighed. "I had to make the first move with your brother. That's not like the boys in Daytona. You give them a smile and they start unzipping their jeans. Then of course if you let them, they call you a slut or whore."

"I'd never do that," I said.

"Good," Ligeia said. "That was a really cool thing about the commune. Girl or guy, if you dig someone and that person digs you, then you get it on. And afterward everyone's cool and nobody puts you down because making it is about sharing."

"I get that," I said. "Free love."

"I think you do, especially the sharing part," Ligeia said, "maybe in a way your brother doesn't."

I smiled.

"I hope so."

The alcohol became an expanding glow, first encircling the two of us, then widening to include the sheltering woods. Ligeia leaned her back against the quilt and beckoned me with her index finger.

"Come lay down with your mermaid."

I did as she asked. Ligeia freed her bikini strap and peeled the cloth away, revealing the pale breasts. I'd always imagined sex as a dim, slow exposure of bodies. Even here in the midafternoon, I'd expected a more subtle unveiling, a turning away, breasts covered with arms and elbows.

"You can look at them," Ligeia said. "I'm not uptight about my body."

She twisted her hips and worked the suit bottom down her legs until she could kick one foot free of the cloth, then the other.

"Now you," Ligeia told me.

My jeans off, I reached in the pocket for the condom.

"Do you know how to put it on?" she asked.

"I think so," I said, but I was so flustered I couldn't open the wrapper. "It's just that I've . . ."

"Hey, everyone has a first time," she said, and took the condom from me. "Lay on your back."

My eyes were open but with my head on the quilt I couldn't see Ligeia, only a gap in the canopy where a single white cloud hung motionless under a blue sky. Her fingers worked the condom down until I was covered.

"Okay," she said, and brought me closer. "Think about something else, like the words to a song. Do that and you'll last longer."

For your first time, you were out of sight," Ligeia said as she slipped her bikini bottom back on.

"You really mean that?" I asked.

"Sure, just as good as your brother, maybe even a bit better."

I pulled my cutoffs up and zipped them.

"How about helping me put my top back on," she said.

I kneeled behind her. As I tied the green strings I thought, now I know what those songs are talking about, I've *done* what they're talking about. Ligeia leaned back onto the quilt and closed her eyes. I did the same but kept my eyes open. The beer and sex, the warm afternoon and the stream's murmur, induced in me a dreamy satedness. I was quite a fine fellow, I told myself, one who wanted nothing more than to be here looking through green leaves at a now-cloudless sky. I was no longer who I'd been, and I'd never be that person, that boy, again.

"So what do you see up there?" Ligeia asked when she opened her eyes.

"I don't know. It just looks nice."

"I see the ocean," she said. "I really must be part mermaid, because if I'm not at the ocean I don't feel at home. Hell, I don't even feel real, at least *all-the-way real*." She laughed softly. "That's a pretty weird thing to say, isn't it? Damn, it's been so long since I've gotten stoned."

"But you'll be living up here until your high school starts?"

"Maybe longer. Now my old man's threatening to make me stay up for my senior year. Either way, as soon as I turn eighteen in October I'm a legal adult and I'll go where I damn well please."

"To the commune?"

"No, Miami. You can make a lot of bread as a cocktail waitress. It's not like Daytona, where the rednecks tip

quarters. But you've got to be eighteen to serve booze."
Ligeia paused. "For once in my life I want to have a few
things of my own, especially my own pad, maybe even
some wheels to go places, and have my kid sister stay
with me some during vacations and summer. I'll take her
shopping and to movies and to eat out, make her feel special, because no one at home will. That was something
that could be a drag at the commune. They said you
were plastic if you were into 'material' things, but most
of them had parents with money. They never had to *give*
something back at the grocery store when everything
was rung up. Your mom ever make you have to do that?"

"No," I answered.

"Well, it's a shitty feeling," Ligeia said. "I never much
believed all that jive about peace and flower power either.
How I grew up, if you didn't scratch and kick when
someone came at you, real bad things could happen."

"Then why do you wear a peace sign?"

"A girl at the commune gave it to me. She said just
wearing it was good karma. That's hippie-dippie dope
talk. But what the hell, I figure wearing it can't hurt,
right?"

"I guess not."

"Don't think I'm putting down the whole commune
scene. I want to go back sometime, but to one in San
Francisco, where every day is a happening. The guy who

rigged up that hip sound system, he says either the Dead or Jefferson Airplane plays a concert every weekend. It's right on the ocean too. Can life get better than that?"

"It sounds really neat," I said.

"And drugs, you can get anything out there," Ligeia said, then smiled. "But hey, what I'm feeling right now ain't bad. Valium is a good vibe anywhere. At the commune most people smoked pot or dropped acid, but I was into floating on downers. Still am."

A white cloud filled the leaf gap, and I imagined the cloud settling beneath me. I wondered if Ligeia had ever seen snow, was about to ask her when she pushed up onto her elbows.

"I need to split soon. Man, I did need a couple of hours away from them. Pretty groovy afternoon for you too, wasn't it?"

"The grooviest," I answered.

"So we should do this again, right?"

"Damn right," I said loudly. "Goddamn right."

Ligeia laughed.

"You're supposed to be the shy brother."

"I'm not so shy."

"No, you're not," she said, and placed her hand on my knee, stroked it lightly. "Your brother though, he's a bit uptight, isn't he, especially about your grandfather?"

"I guess so," I said. "Grandfather's pretty strict."

"Bill says he won't get me any more Valium."

"I know."

"And you're okay with that?" Ligeia asked.

"I guess so."

"Because Bill decides things for both of you?"

"He doesn't decide anything for me."

Ligeia smiled.

"I bet your grandfather has samples galore in his office."

"He has a lot," I admitted.

"He won't know and Bill won't have to know if you get your mermaid something to feel good, right?"

"I guess not," I said after a few moments.

"You could try them too," she said, moving closer, her breath in my ear. "So what do you say, Eugene? You'll be a real sweetheart if you do."

"Okay," I said softly.

She kissed me on the mouth.

"You won't change your mind, will you?"

"No, but don't tell Bill."

"I don't fink on people," she said, getting up. "This is our secret."

When we walked upstream, Bill smiled but didn't say anything.

"Can I take the rest of the wine?" Ligeia asked. "I can stash it behind my uncle's shed."

"Sure," Bill said.

"And next Sunday, how about bringing some cigarettes? Aunt Cazzie and Uncle Hiram would flip out completely if I asked for some."

"What kind of cigarettes?" I asked.

"Virginia Slims. I'll pay you back."

"Okay," I said.

"I'd better split or they'll think I drowned," Ligeia said.

I found the wine-bottle cap and handed it to her.

"Thanks," she said, kissing my cheek before she turned to Bill. "Your brother's a quick learner."

As she crossed the stream, Bill pulled the stringer from the water; three trout dangled from it now instead of two.

"This will be enough to keep on the old man's good side," he said, freeing the smallest fish and reaching for the Ka-Bar knife he sharpened after every fishing trip before pocketing it. The blade tip settled on the trout's abdomen and in one quick motion the flesh opened like scissored silk. I turned away, feeling queasy again.

"I'll load the truck while you clean them," I said.

I finished before Bill and waited inside the cab. A dull pain settled in the back of my head. Maybe just two next time, I told myself. I heard Bill tramping through the laurel, then a rattling thunk when he threw the stringer into the truck bed.

"You okay?" Bill asked. "You look a bit green around the gills. You guzzled those beers and that's not smart. You didn't puke while you were with Ligeia, did you?"

"No."

"You're lucky. The first time I drank beer I did three and hugged a commode for an hour."

Maybe I can hold my alcohol better than you, I thought, smiling to myself as Bill cranked the engine.

The bumpy drive up the logging road unsettled my stomach, but once on the four-lane I rolled my window down and felt better. The cool wind seemed to lessen my headache too. I turned on the radio.

"So how was it?" Bill asked as I searched through the static for a station.

"The beer tasted good."

"I could tell that by how much you drank," Bill snorted. "I meant the other thing."

I twisted the dial and finally found a clear station, but it was playing Merle Haggard.

"Assuming it happened," Bill added.

"It happened," I answered, then more sharply, "and it was damn good for me and for her. I was every bit as good as you were, probably better. She told me so."

"Okay, okay, I believe you," Bill said. "Damn, you don't have to get on your high horse about it."

I'd found another station and turned up the volume. I didn't recognize the song, but it wasn't country. Then "Good Lovin'" came on and I sang along. *Baby please squeeze me tight.* Yeah, I know what that's about, I thought, and sang louder. I've *done* what they're singing about. Did it damn well too.

CHAPTER NINE

It was almost noon on the following Wednesday when Ligeia's uncle Hiram came through the office's front door.

"Oh, shit," Bill whispered as Mr. Mosely stepped up to Shirley's window and asked to see Grandfather.

Like sprinters ready to bolt, we both leaned forward, eyes lowered. Then Mr. Mosely raised a hand wrapped in a bloody handkerchief. Shirley told him to have a seat. He turned and saw me and nodded. I returned the nod and picked up a magazine, relieved when he sat near the door. Soon a patient came out and Shirley told Mr. Mosely he could go on back. A few minutes later Grandfather called Bill to join them.

"It's not about her," Bill said, but looked uneasy as he stood.

I followed Bill but stopped in the hallway. The room's door remained open. Mr. Mosely sat on the steel examination table, his gashed palm tinted orange with Betadine.

"You won't object if Bill does the stitching, will you?" Grandfather said. "He'll do a better job than I can."

"No, sir."

"Go ahead, Bill," Grandfather said. "Three should be enough."

Bill threaded the needle and Mr. Mosely laid his hand palm up on the table, wincing as Bill completed the first stitch.

"I've heard your brother's daughter is here for the summer," Grandfather said.

Mr. Mosely nodded.

"Because she got into trouble with the law," Grandfather added as Bill's needle paused. "Is that right?"

"She has, but Jimmy said it's mainly her running around with the wrong crowd. That's why she's up here."

"Is she giving you any trouble?" Grandfather asked.

"No, sir, but Cazzie and me don't let her go out," Mr. Mosely said, clenching his teeth as Bill pulled the needle through the second time, "unless one of us is with her."

"Is it not numb enough?" Bill asked.

"It's numb enough," Grandfather said. "Finish it."

"I'm all right," Mr. Mosely told Bill.

"A tight leash is what you need with a teenager like that," Grandfather said as Bill completed the third stitch and knotted the thread. "Hold it up, Mosely."

He raised his hand and Grandfather inspected it.

"You'll not find better stitching on a Major League baseball," Grandfather said. "Wait a week then clip the stitches and pull them out."

"Yes, sir," Mr. Mosely said.

"I hope you've learned your lesson about being careless around saw blades," Grandfather said. "We don't stitch limbs back on, do we, Bill?"

"No, sir," Bill said, setting the needle and thread on a steel tray.

"For a moment there I thought we were in some deep shit," Bill said when Mr. Mosely had paid and left. "This settles one thing for certain. There's no way we're taking as much as an aspirin out of that closet again. I can't believe that I was stupid enough to do it even once."

But I had already done so, on the previous afternoon when Bill and I were cleaning up. When he went into Grandfather's office to mop, I opened the closet and fumbled through the various samples and packets.

I found a Valium packet just as I heard the office's front door open. I'd barely closed the closet door and jammed the Valium in my pocket when Nebo came into the hallway. He stepped past me and leaned over the water fountain, gulping and then coughing each time he raised his glistening bulb of a head. I went to the other closet and got a mop and bucket. I remembered the love beads then, the ones I'd bought Monday night and dared not wear in Grandfather's presence. I tucked them deeper under my collar but when I came back down the hall Nebo was gone.

"So you were at the office too when Uncle Hiram showed up?" Ligeia said after we'd made love the following Sunday.

"I was there."

"Bill acts like he didn't sweat it, but I bet you guys almost flipped out."

I smiled, feeling the buzz of three beers, thinking *Buzz Buzz Buzz,* if this feeling were a sound it would be that: bees hovering.

"I didn't."

"But Bill did?"

"He did until he saw your uncle's hand."

"Uncle Hiram was showing off those stitches like they were made out of gold. It sounds like everyone in

Sylva thinks Bill is the second coming of Christ. I bet that gets old, hearing it all the time."

"It does get old, but you seem to be the only person who realizes it."

"Hey, but you're the one who wasn't too chicken to get my head candy," Ligeia said, nodding at the empty packet. "Even Uncle Hiram says your grandfather is a real hardass. Yeah, you've got your brother beat in the balls department, no doubt about that, Eugene. Bill wouldn't dare wear those beads you have on either, would he?"

"No way," I answered. "He keeps saying Grandfather's going to wring my neck if he sees them on me."

Ligeia ran a fingertip over my beads, her sharp nail lightly raking my skin.

"They look great on you, Eugene."

I smiled because I'd checked in the bathroom mirror before Bill and I left the house and for once I'd liked what I'd seen.

"I've got a present for you," I said, and reached into my pants pocket.

"They're the same colors as yours," Ligeia said, smiling as she placed the beads over the ones already on her neck. "Where'd you get them? Don't tell me there's a head shop here in Hicksville?"

"In Waynesville," I answered. "I drove over there Monday night."

"There's a head shop there?"

"I guess that's what it is," I answered. "It's real new. They have incense, beads, Day-Glo posters, and some really good albums, the Grateful Dead, Jefferson Airplane, almost every group you told me about. If I had something to play them on, I would have bought a couple."

"Why don't you buy a stereo?" Ligeia asked. "Grandpa pays you for working, doesn't he?"

"He puts the money in our bank accounts. Until I'm eighteen he has to co-sign, and he won't let me take out more than twenty-five a week."

"How much do you have in there?"

"Right at two thousand."

"Damn, sweetheart. You can buy an out-of-sight stereo for three hundred. He won't let you spend your own dough?"

"There's no way," I said. "Not for that sort of thing. Of course Bill can, and he's got more money than me, but he's not into music enough to buy a stereo."

"That's a bummer," Ligeia said, "but a head shop being around here is pretty cool. I talked to my sis last night. She's coming up and is bringing some pot with her. I bet they've got pipes and wrapping papers there. You ever smoked pot?"

"No, a beer buzz works fine for me."

"Pot's okay, but what you got me is waaaay better. When I get some pot, I'll bring it. What about the Valium? You didn't get some for yourself?"

"I have to be careful not to get too much," I answered. "I want you to have it."

"You're so sweet," she said, and reached behind her for a dollar bill. "Oh, yeah, I forgot to give you this, for the cigarettes. Next time I'll help with the wine too. Bill said you made a big deal about paying for it."

"I don't want the money," I said, and paused. "This could be kind of a date, couldn't it? I mean, if that's okay."

"A date," Ligeia said. "You still do that up here?"

"Yes."

She shook her head, then gave a soft laugh.

"All right," she said, smiling as she laid the money beside the quilt, "but you've missed out on the necking and slipping your hands under my bra and panties and all that other 'date' stuff. You skipped first, second, and third base and scored right away."

A pleasant prickling spread over my face and scalp.

"I'm not complaining a bit," I said.

"Do I have to date your brother too?"

"Do you mean William Gaylord Matney the Third?" I answered, and grinned. "No, just me."

"Oh, God," Ligeia giggled. "Is that really his full name?"

"Really."

"He doesn't ever call himself that, does he?"

"He does when he's at school," I lied. "I laugh at him any time he uses it around me."

"Good for you," she said, and began giggling again. "I knew he was uptight but he's always been nice enough, and he does get us the beer and wine, but God it's going to be hard to ever look him in the face again without laughing."

"One time he signed a check with William Matney the Third on it," I said, lying again, "and I changed it to where it read William Matney the Turd."

Ligeia's giggle turned into a harsh laugh, almost a barking sound.

"You're really funny," she said when she stopped. "I like that."

"So we can call it a date?" I said.

"Okay then," Ligeia said. "We can 'date.' Just remember that flowers and boxes of chocolates aren't what turn this chick on, right?"

"Right," I answered.

For the rest of June, we rendezvoused with Ligeia on Sunday afternoons. When Bill was doing a procedure with Grandfather, I went to the closet and stole Valium or Quaalude samples. On Sundays Bill stopped at the convenience store. He paid for the beer but I paid for the Strawberry Hill wine. Bill got the condoms from a machine in the restroom, but I put the coins in the cigarette machine and pulled the knob for Virginia Slims. Each week I hoped Ligeia might not let Bill join her in the woods. It's only because Bill's buying us the alcohol, isn't it, I wanted to ask, but I didn't. It wasn't until Leslie visited in July that things began to change.

CHAPTER TEN

The day after visiting Bill in Asheville, I awake to a knocking at my front door. I go to the window and see Sheriff Loudermilk's squad car. A coincidence, I try to tell myself, just another complaint about uncut grass or empty garbage cans. But I know it's not that, and I realize something else—a part of me has been awaiting this visit.

Cotton mouthed and half stumbling, I grab a dingy bathrobe and move toward the door. I walk into the front room where late-morning sun slants through the blinds, awakening a headache I'd hoped to sleep through. Dust motes drift in the yellow light, bringing back a moment of childhood, more sensation than memory, of a tall shadow thickening over me and then a weightless rising. The knocking becomes more insistent.

"I need to talk to you," Robbie Loudermilk says when I open the door.

"If it's about the grass," I answer, my hand on the doorknob, "I'll get it cut."

"It's not about that. Mind if I come in?"

"As you can see, Sheriff, I haven't gotten dressed."

"I don't mind waiting until you do."

My hand's still on the knob. The brass is cold and dense, suddenly real in a way nothing else quite is.

"So can I come in or not, Mr. Matney?"

I open the door wider. Loudermilk stoops as he enters, a tall drink of water, as older folks used to say. His hair is suspiciously black for a man well over sixty and he wears it roached back like a TV preacher. All of it, including the poorly reset nose and clenched smile, seem part of his uniform.

"I played on that ball team with your brother," Loudermilk says, stepping closer to the mantel. "I was pretty good, but Bill was on a way other level. And now he's a big-time surgeon. A lot of people aren't very good at even one thing. Matter of fact, some are just world-class fuck-ups," he adds, still looking at the photograph. "They can't keep a job, or a family. Hell, they can't even drive sober with their own child in the car."

He turns and bares a set of teeth white as porcelain. It seems incongruous, even a liability when dealing with the rough sorts who'd consider artificially whitened teeth effete.

"I counted Bill a friend in high school, even came here to visit a few times. Your mother always had milk and cookies for us. Of course, this house was kept up better then. Doesn't seem to be a priority for you. Yeah, Bill was my buddy, until he hired his hotshot lawyer to get you off. That changed things."

"I need to get dressed, Sheriff, so if you don't mind . . ."

"Go ahead," Loudermilk says. "I'm in no hurry."

I go upstairs and put on a sweatshirt and jeans. When I return, he's gazing at the photos, which gives me a moment to scan the room. A plastic cup, an empty wine bottle, and a dwindling fifth of Jack Daniel's crowd the lamp table. On the floor by the couch, a dusty scatter of books and magazines. And on the couch itself, something I quickly look away from.

"Your mother was an attractive woman," Loudermilk says as he turns. "It's surprising she never remarried. I used to see her when I took my grandkids to the library. She always took time with them, suggesting books, that kind of thing."

I step closer to the front door, hoping his eyes if not his feet will follow.

"What is it you wanted to see me about, Sheriff?"

"Ligeia Mosely. You knew her in high school, right?"

"I think so."

"You think so?"

"Yes, she wasn't a friend or anything. I just knew who she was."

"Who she *was*," Loudermilk says. "So you know they found her body over at Panther Creek?"

"I read about it in the paper."

"I noticed," he tells me, and nods at the folded newspaper. *Remains Identified* is at the top in bold black. "So she wasn't a friend?"

"Like I told you, Sheriff, I knew who she was."

"But not someone you ever hung out with?"

"That's right," I answer.

"Angie Wellbeck says otherwise."

"Angie Wellbeck?"

"She was a high school friend of Ligeia's until they had a falling-out. After we asked for information, Angie came to see me. According to her, you and Ligeia were up to something that involved you giving her money. Angie didn't know exactly how much, but she did say it was a wad of bills, and the one on the outside was a twenty."

"I don't know . . ."

Loudermilk raises a hand.

"Angie admitted that Ligeia was selling drugs, but using more than she sold. That's why they had a falling-out, Ligeia borrowing money she wouldn't pay back. Or couldn't pay back, because she owed money to other people."

"I don't know anything about that."

"You need a drink?" Loudermilk asks. "You seem a little shaky."

"Why are you here, Sheriff?"

"Just curious about why you'd give Ligeia Mosely money."

"I didn't give her any money."

"Why would Angie Wellbeck lie about that?"

"I don't know," I answer, speaking slowly to steady my voice. "It was forty-six years ago. She must be confusing me with someone else."

"No, Angie was certain it was you. She said you had zits and blond hair and were skinny as a scarecrow. The pimples are gone, by there's yet some blond in that gray hair of yours. And you're still not exactly Mr. Universe, are you?"

"She's mistaken, Sheriff. I'm sorry Ligeia Mosely's dead but it's got nothing to do with me."

Loudermilk rubs the back of his neck. He looks above me, then resettles his eyes on mine.

"I almost sent one of my deputies to talk to you, but I came out of respect for your mother. Now I'm glad I came. We know Ligeia was arrested for possessing prescription drugs in Daytona Beach, right before she came up here, and after what Angie Wellbeck told me, I figured this was about a dealer she owed money to, a dealer from Daytona, because she kept telling Angie that she was going to Miami, not Daytona. I hoped as a customer you might lead me to someone who might know someone. That kind of thing. But now . . ."

I start to speak but Loudermilk doesn't let me.

"Here's the thing, Matney. Ever since I got here you've been nervous as a cat in a room full of rocking chairs. And your newspaper turned to a story about her, that's a tad curious, don't you think? Look, I didn't come here to accuse you of anything, but I owe it to the Mosely family to get the truth of what happened."

"I said I knew who she was."

"You sure you don't need a drink?" Loudermilk says. "It might loosen you up to remember some things. I'm not a drinking man myself, but I understand lots of times a man drinks to forget. I mean, look at you, your brother and grandfather both doctors and here you are, holed up drinking away your life. Maybe there's something you want to forget involving Ligeia Mosely."

"You've been reading too many pop psychology books, Sheriff."

"No, this is my own thinking, but you're probably right. Any man driving drunk with his own daughter in the car can't be troubled too much about hurting people."

"Is that what all of this is about, Sheriff, my DUI charge? Charge, not conviction."

"I didn't like you getting off," he answers, "but I've learned a slick enough lawyer can always find a technicality. I bet it was a pretty penny your brother paid him though. But no, it's not about DUIs. It's about why someone cut the throat of a seventeen-year-old girl."

Loudermilk stops and stares at me intently.

"You're surprised," he says softly.

Surprised, yes, but even more the sudden sense of weightlessness when a trapdoor's sprung. For a few moments neither of us speaks.

"I'm surprised because all I know about any of this is what the newspaper said."

"And what was that?" Loudermilk asks.

"That the cause of death hadn't been confirmed."

"That was before forensics in Raleigh had a look. A sharp-bladed instrument, maybe a knife, maybe not, cut into her upper spine so deep it damn near cut her head off. Anyway, let's get back to the money you gave her. It was for drugs, right?"

"I didn't give her any money," I answer, "for drugs or anything else."

"Be careful, Matney, you're acting guilty again, and right when I thought you might not know anything after all. Look, you know I can't charge you for buying drugs that long ago. But the statute of limitations doesn't apply to murder. So a name or names, even if you think they had nothing to do with this. That's all I want from you."

"I don't know anything about any of this, Sheriff."

"Then why did you give her money?"

"I didn't give her money. Her friend is wrong."

Loudermilk tilts his head ever so slightly. He's not a stupid man, but nowhere as clever as he thinks. The lawyer had made that clear at my DUI trial. By the time he'd finished, Loudermilk had contradicted himself a dozen times. He nods at the Jack Daniel's bottle.

"Okay, you've probably wiped out enough brain cells not to remember," he says. "You been drinking this morning?"

"No."

"Too bad. I wish you'd empty that bottle and get in your car, because if I catch you again, even the damn governor won't be able to help you. I'll make sure every newspaper in the state knows about it, and about what happened the last time. And I won't spare Bill. He was wrong to get your worthless ass off, even if you are his brother."

Loudermilk lifts his right hand and flexes an open palm sideways, the way people once hit typewriter return bars. It's an odd gesture, perhaps one of dismissiveness, like moving on to a new paragraph, a new topic. He lowers the hand.

"There are a couple of other folks Angie Wellbeck suggested I contact," he says, "guys Ligeia knew, rough sorts. Sylva's a small town, and small towns have a way of eventually giving up their secrets. I may find out from someone else that you're tied to this, and that may lead to an obstruction of justice charge, so if there's something you 'forgot' to tell me, or you want to get off your chest, call me."

Loudermilk walks out the door and drives off. Sweat trickles down my spine. My forehead glistens, which Loudermilk surely noticed. I stare at the bottle of Jack Daniel's. One drink and by law I'm still sober, so I splash a shot glass's worth of whiskey into the plastic cup. My hand trembles as I raise the cup to my mouth but I do not swallow yet. Instead, I close my eyes and let the liquor's soft burn flood over my tongue. I level my chin and inhale through my nose, savor the peaty aftertaste on the back of my mouth and upper throat as I slowly swallow.

Leonardo's disembodied hand comes to me with an almost hallucinatory intensity, beckons me back to a childhood afternoon when Bill pressed a blade into my flesh and cut. He was twelve and I seven. A long-abandoned house, supposedly haunted, lay behind the county rec center. One afternoon after Bill and I had gone swimming, Bill wanted to explore it. I didn't want to go but Bill coerced me with the promise of a milk shake at Pike's Drugstore. I was following him up the porch steps when a shard of rotten wood lodged in my foot.

"You knew better than to be in that old house," Grandfather said when Bill helped me into the office. "You're damn lucky a board didn't give and break some bones."

"I'm sorry," Bill said.

"That's not good enough, son," Grandfather answered as I waited on the examination table, injured foot flexed, watching with dread as Grandfather set the tray of bright, sinister instruments on the counter. After he called Shirley back to prepare the lidocaine shot, Grandfather handed Bill gauze and a bottle of Betadine. "Clean around that wound," he told him.

Bill hesitated, then soaked the gauze and gingerly coated my tender mid-foot, pausing each time I winced. Shirley handed Grandfather the needle and syringe as Bill dropped the gauze in the wastebasket and set the Betadine on the counter.

"You're not finished," Grandfather said, and placed the syringe in Bill's right hand.

"I've never given a shot," Bill stammered.

"Good," Grandfather said. "You'll learn several lessons today."

"No, sir, I can't," Bill said. "I don't know how to."

"You've seen it done," Grandfather scoffed.

"I know you need to deaden all around it," Bill said, "but I don't know how deep to go, or how much in each place."

"If you don't go deep enough, son," Grandfather said coldly, "I'll tell you and you can do it again. If it's not enough, you will know that pretty quick."

Bill turned to Shirley, hoping she'd offer to do it, though he knew as well as I that she'd no more defy Grandfather than Nebo would.

"The foot has to be lanced to get that splinter out, and you can lance it with or without lidocaine," Grandfather said, turning to me. "Do you want your brother to do it with or without numbing it?"

I said I wanted my mother, and between wiping tears off my face pleaded that the splinter didn't hurt anymore and I wanted it left in. Grandfather lifted the steel lance from the tray, nodded at the syringe in Bill's hand.

"Your choice, boys?" Grandfather said.

Shirley took a needle and syringe from a cabinet.

"Like this, Bill," she said, and angled the needle into her upper arm. "See, just under the skin." Shirley slowly withdrew the needle. She angled it again, an inch higher on her arm, and repierced the skin. "Do that twice on each side, a quarter of a centimeter of the lidocaine in each place."

Bill nodded, but uncertainty clouded his face as he came over to me. "Close your eyes and keep your foot as still as you can, Eugene. Pinch your arm the way I showed you at the dentist," he added. "That way you'll hardly feel it."

I did what he said. The needle still hurt though, and I tried to jerk my leg back. Bill clamped his hands on my ankle. For a sickening moment, I felt the needle dangle from my foot, free of Bill's grasp. Then he secured it and injected the lidocaine around the skin.

"Quit being such a sissy," Grandfather barked. "You hear me, boy?"

I opened my eyes, thinking he scolded me but Grandfather's glare was aimed at Bill, whose eyes, for the only time I ever saw in our childhood or adolescence, had filled with tears. But unlike my own, Bill quickly stanched his with a wrist rubbed over his eyes. He set the needle and syringe in the metal tray, and when Grandfather held out the scalpel, Bill took it. I looked away, only to see the disembodied hand raised above us as if to bless the proceedings.

"Quit crying, Eugene, and close your eyes," my brother said quietly. "It won't hurt, I promise."

I closed my eyes but I couldn't keep my body from shaking.

"You've got to be still, Eugene," Bill said, settling his free hand on my ankle. "Feel that?"

"Feel what?" I answered.

"It's out," Bill said moments later and I opened my eyes.

He held up a bloody inch-long wood shard.

"Are you certain you got it all?" Grandfather asked.

"Yes, sir," Bill replied.

I watched him wipe off the scalpel with gauze and set it back in the tray. Grandfather came over and inspected the cut.

"Well done," he told my brother. "The patient should survive."

Despite Bill telling me not to call his office, I do anyway.

"Dr. Matney cannot come to the phone," the receptionist says.

"Where is he?"

"I'm not at liberty to say."

"I'm his fucking brother, in case you haven't forgotten."

"I'm following orders," the receptionist answers, "his orders."

"I need to know where he is and I need to know *now*, damn it."

"Mr. Matney, I'm going to have to hang up."

"Listen," I say, trying not to shout. "You tell him to call me right now, that I *will* see him, even if I have to come into his operating room. Do you understand?"

"Yes," she hisses, and then all I hear is a dial tone. Though I place the phone back in the cradle, my hand remains on it. I think of Sarah's photograph and how her coat befitted a northern city. But which one . . . Boston, New York, Hartford?

There is a moment in Nabokov's novel *Lolita* when the title character explains her mother's demise with two words: "Picnic/Lightning," thus hurdling a scene that Nabokov's character and the writer himself, no doubt, found too tedious to explain further. At the final AA meetings I went to, "Family/Alcohol" would have sufficed. But I told my story, explaining what had been lost: the academic, perhaps even literary, career; a teaching job; the marriage. I never spoke about Sarah though. To do so seemed a surrender of hope. But there was another reason. Nietzsche once said "that for which we find words is something already dead in our hearts." I didn't believe that, but to willfully defy the quote was to tempt fate—and if to find it true, to know nothing remained but emptiness.

CHAPTER ELEVEN

It was a Friday in mid-July when Leslie drove the six hours from Virginia to Sylva. The photograph I'd seen had not done her justice, especially her eyes, their ripe blueberry color but also their almond shape. Taller than I'd thought as well, five ten or so. She was shy and tended to hunch slightly when nervous, perhaps because, like most tall girls in adolescence, she'd towered over both genders, so wished to appear smaller. Knowing she'd once doubted her own attractiveness made me like her even more. My mother warmed to her immediately. Leslie was given my bedroom and I slept on the couch. On Saturday she and Bill spent the day on the Blue Ridge Parkway, taking with them a picnic lunch our mother made. So I polished the office floors without Bill, but I didn't work by myself. Nebo, seeing I was alone, grunted and took the buffer from my hands.

I sat in the waiting room while Nebo finished, his huge hands guiding the metal disk across the floor, working without pause until the last room was done. When he was through, he put the machine back in the closet and sat down in a chair across from me. He wiped a phlegm-stained handkerchief across his brow and then over a skull made red from the exertion. I'd never been alone with Nebo before and it was unsettling. I had the key so I flipped through a magazine, waiting for him to leave. When I set the magazine back down ten minutes later, he hadn't moved.

"I guess I'd better lock up," I told him, but Nebo didn't acknowledge my words. He continued to sit with his legs apart, forearms resting on his knees. I could see the outlines of the razor and whetstone in his front-right pocket and recalled a particularly frightening childhood dream of that razor. "I had better lock up," I said louder, and when he still didn't move added, "Grandfather doesn't like me to be here if I'm not working." He stood and went outside. When I heard the whir of the push mower, I went to the closet and, since the decreasing Valium samples might soon be noticed, pocketed two Quaalude packets.

Despite Leslie's long drive back to Virginia, Grandfather insisted she stay for Sunday lunch. We all went to church together but it was only when we arrived at Grandfather's house that the interrogation began. He asked Leslie about her family and her plans after college. Her answers, father a Methodist minister, mother a housewife, like her plans to be a lab technician, elicited a tight-lipped nod, as if, as my brother seethed later that day, Leslie were a hunting dog whose lineage was being appraised.

Maybe if it had ended there, nothing more would have happened, because though Leslie's hunched posture implied tension, she answered courteously. Grandfather then held forth on how medical students shouldn't marry until at least their residency, and how he was sure Bill had explained this to her. My mother tried to change the subject, but Grandfather stopped her with a glare. Bill had stared silently at his plate through most of it, though he took Leslie's hand once the questioning began. It was when Grandfather spoke of children being unwise for sleep-deprived residents that Bill set his hands against the table as if ready to upturn it onto Grandfather. His arms shook and his face filled with the same fury as when he'd been cleated.

"What Leslie and I decide about our future is none of your business, Grandfather," Bill said.

For only the second time I know of, our grandfather appeared astonished.

"Well, Bill," he sputtered, "I don't mean to . . ."

Then Grandfather's face and body pulled taut. It was like watching a startled copperhead coil to strike.

"It is indeed my business, boy, if I'm paying for your education," he said, "and you had better never, ever, forget that."

Bill pushed back his chair and stood.

"Leslie needs to go," he said, taking Leslie's arm to urge her up too. After a few strained good-byes we left. Back at our house, my brother carried Leslie's suitcase to her car, where they lingered despite the midday heat. I watched from my bedroom window as they talked. It was a serious conversation, followed by a fervent kiss. Bill still wore his suit, and as Leslie drove away, my brother wiped the back of his wrist across his brow, or perhaps across his eyes.

"Can you believe he did that?" Bill fumed an hour later as we drove toward Panther Creek.

Of course I could, and said so.

"I should go over there right now and call him an asshole to his face," Bill said. "That old man shouldn't be allowed to live his whole life without someone doing it at least once."

I'd have enjoyed watching Bill do that, but Ligeia was waiting for us. I turned the radio on. A James Taylor song played and I kept it there, hoping it might mellow Bill out. At the convenience store he got the beer and the Strawberry Hill, but he told me if I wanted a condom to buy it myself. I went to the restroom and got one from the machine clamped to the wall.

When we got to Panther Creek, Ligeia was sitting by the big pool. Bill didn't bother with the rods and reels. He tore a beer from the plastic and walked upstream. I got a beer for myself and opened the wine and filled a cup.

"What's bumming your brother out?" Ligeia asked as she took the wine.

"He's pissed at our grandfather."

I pulled the beer tab, a sound I looked forward to more and more. It was like an exhaled breath I'd been holding since the last Sunday. I set the rest in the creek and took a long swallow.

"He's far enough away not to see the candy you brought your sweetheart," Ligeia said.

I dug the Quaalude samples out of my pocket and handed them to her.

"The Valium was getting low."

"These are even better," Ligeia said, opening one packet and washing the white tablets down with the wine. "Plenty of these, though, right?"

"Some."

"Thanks for getting me some extra again," she said, gesturing at the second packet. "Getting stoned is the only way I make it through Wednesday-night prayer service. Too bad I don't have three packets. If I did, your mermaid could float through Sunday school and preaching too."

Ligeia paused and looked upstream. Bill was out of sight now.

"I need to ask you something," Ligeia said. "My sis is coming up here Saturday and she's bringing weed with her, a lot of it. There are kids around here who smoke pot, right?"

"Yes, some," I said.

"Good, I need money for Miami, not just to get there but for an apartment down payment, that kind of thing. If I do end up here until October, maybe I could clear a thousand. That's enough until I get my first paycheck. Jimmy, the guy my sis is getting the pot from, he can get me as much as I can sell. You know, Eugene," Ligeia said more softly, "I could deal more than pot. I bet there's all sorts of goodies in that cabinet. Dexedrine, Obetrol, Desoxyn. We could split the profit, if you're okay with it."

"I'd get caught for sure if I did that."

"Just a thought," Ligeia said. "Jimmy can get me some. He can get anything. Last summer he could score downers as easy as at the commune. We had a blast until we got busted."

"You and Jimmy, are you good friends?"

A trout rose in the pool's center, sipped an insect off the surface. Ligeia moved closer, placed a finger in a jeans loop and gave a tug.

"Why don't you get the quilt," she said, lifting the wine bottle off the bank. "I'll meet you downstream. I'm going to do something new to you, and I think you'll really dig it."

I took the quilt from the truck bed. The rods would stay there, unless Bill wanted to try and make peace with Grandfather. I took two beers from the creek and joined her.

Ligeia still wore her bathing suit. I lay down beside her and was taking the condom from my pocket when she pressed her hand to mine.

"You won't need that," she said. "Just lie back, Eugene. I'll do the rest."

Afterward, we lay beside each other awhile, then she raised herself onto her elbows. I did the same, drinking my third beer while she sipped wine. When my can was empty, she passed me the half-filled bottle.

"I don't want anymore, so you drink the rest."

"Sure," I said, and raised the bottle to my mouth.

I didn't like the sweet taste but took another long swallow.

"You don't like it, do you?"

"Not really, but like you say, it gets the job done."

"We need the hard stuff," Ligeia said. "I bet your grandfather drinks some high-dollar whiskey. You ought to cop us a bottle."

"He doesn't drink."

"You're bullshitting me?"

"No, he doesn't."

"What a waste," Ligeia said. "To have money and not use it to feel good. And talk about feeding your head, he can get pills that will take him up, down, or sideways, gets them *free*, and he doesn't touch them?"

"No," I answered. "He'd never do that."

"I bet he's got a fancy house, though, right?"

"It's nice."

"I'd never want that," she said, sounding wistful, "but a cozy little beach house right on the ocean, that would be out of sight."

"Maybe you will have one," I said, but Ligeia didn't seem to hear me. She stared out at the woods.

The wine had taken my buzz up another notch. I took another swallow. Cough syrup, the red kind, I thought.

"Why don't you go get Bill," Ligeia said. "Tell him I'll help him get over his pouting."

"It's probably better if I don't," I said. "When he gets in a bad mood like this, he stays in it."

"Go ask him anyway."

I got up slowly, feeling the full effect of the beer and wine for a few dizzying moments, then made my way upstream. Bill was at the pool, a beer can settled on a kneecap as he sat and stared at the water.

"Ligeia wanted to know if you were over your pouting yet."

"I'm not pouting," Bill answered, "and I'm not going over to where she is either."

"Why not?" I asked.

"I'm just not."

"What do you want me to tell her?"

"You don't have to tell her anything except that I'm not doing what we've been doing ever again."

"Okay," I said, and nodded at the single beer left in the creek. "You going to drink it?"

"No," Bill answered, "but you shouldn't either. It's clear you've had more than enough already."

I took the beer from the stream and walked into the woods.

"Just because he's pissed at your grandfather?" Ligeia asked when I told her.

"I think it's more because his girlfriend at college came to see him this weekend."

"So she wore him out?"

"I don't know," I said. "They're pretty serious. I mean, he said he wasn't going to . . . you know, with you anymore."

"Well, that is William's hang-up," she said, "not ours, right?"

"Right," I answered. "He acts like he's forty years old. If I crank up the radio, he complains more than our mom."

Ligeia lay back and closed her eyes. I closed mine too.

"I like this," I said, "it being just me and you."

"You and me is groovy," Ligeia said. "Bill's got some good things going for him, but he can get boring. He talks about medicine and science, even baseball, for God's sake. The books you tell me about are cool, even if I haven't read them, and talking music with you is a blast, unlike with your brother. Can you believe the music he's into? Simon and Garfunkel? That's like listening to Lawrence Welk."

"Yeah," I agreed. "It's lame."

"Anyway," Ligeia said. "He'd better not try to hang some guilt trip on me."

"Damn right," I agreed, loud enough that Bill might hear, "the hell with William the Third."

I emptied the wine bottle with a long last swallow, held it by the neck, and threw it in a looping arc toward the creek. It hit a rock and shattered.

"Why the hell did you do that?" Ligeia bristled. "I could get a goddamn gash in my foot from that."

"Don't worry," I said, grinning. "William's going to be a world-renowned surgeon. He can sew you up with fishing line."

Even through the alcohol haze I knew it was a stupid thing to say, as the look on Ligeia's face made clear.

"I need to split," she said, and got up.

"Hey," I said, feeling the world waver as I also stood. "I'm sorry. I very am."

"I *very* am?"

"I really am," I answered. "I'm real sorry. It was stupid."

"Okay," Ligeia said after a few seconds.

"You'll come back next week, won't you?"

She looked at me and her eyes faded back into their druggy dreaminess.

"Sure," she said. "But you'll still bring your mermaid her feel-good pills, right, maybe a couple of extra if you can?"

"Yes," I said.

I walked with her to the creek, though I was the one barefoot.

"Next week, then," Ligeia said, and waded into the water.

My brother was true to his word. After Leslie visited, Bill never joined Ligeia in the woods. Besides paying for the wine, I bought her presents with my allowance, trinkets really, a copper bracelet with LUV stamped on it, a ring with a yellow smiley face. *My girlfriend*, that was how I thought of her. Sometimes in front of the mirror I'd say it out loud, and when I listened to the radio the love songs made me think that maybe I was in love. "That's sweet of you," she'd say with each gift, but except for the beads she never wore them afterward. Ligeia said she hid them in her suitcase so her uncle and aunt wouldn't wonder where they came from.

Bill kept working at my grandfather's office, but the strain between them was palpable. If Grandfather wouldn't have stopped anyone else in Sylva from hiring him, Bill probably would have quit. For two more Sundays, my brother went with me to Panther Creek, but he clearly didn't enjoy himself. As soon as we arrived, Bill sat on the bank with a beer in his hand. He didn't swim or fish and stopped at two beers. That was fine since it gave me one more, which I drank though he said I should stop at three, not knowing I drank half the wine too. Acting like a babysitter, thinking he *was* my babysitter.

One night, unbidden, Bill explained what had changed. *Seeing Leslie again, I realized how wrong being with Ligeia was. It's disrespectful and it would hurt her if she ever found out. I want to marry her.* Less than a year later my brother did. As Bill and I waited in an anteroom for the wedding to begin, he'd told me why. *She makes me a better person than I really am,* my brother said.

CHAPTER TWELVE

An hour after Sheriff Loudermilk leaves, my brother hasn't called. I've resisted another drink but knowing the bottle is an arm's length away is too tempting so I get my keys and drive to Bill's office. All the while, memories flip like calendars in old movies, blurring events, blurring time. I try to center on a single thought, confirm its solidity, the way I'd test boards on a rickety porch. *My brother has lied to me.* This is true, because Ligeia died from a slashed throat, not drowning. *But why would my brother lie to me?* The obvious answer: *Because my brother is a murderer.* But I don't know *how* to believe such a thing. The man I know now could not have done that. *But he's not now who he was then.* And to bury her there, the cruelty of that, especially for Ligeia's family. Bill had bruised my feelings at times, but how many times deliberately? Even the teasing stopped when he saw I was truly upset. We never fought and rarely engaged in the rough horseplay brothers so often get into. His anger at Grandfather and at the player who'd cleated him were instinctive responses to provocations. Didn't any act of cruelty require a degree of calculation?

But then a memory of another baseball game. Bill was pitching and in the first inning a batter hit a home run, the first he had given up all season. Bill looked stunned as the batter trotted the bases, as if thinking: *How dare you. Don't you know who I am and who I'm going to be?* Maybe the batter did something more, a smirk as he tapped the plate, an under-the-breath taunt. I don't know. What I do know is when the batter came up again, Bill threw right at his head, forcing him to dive to the dirt. The umpire and Bill's coach rushed to the mound. The coach threatened to send Bill to the dugout, and the umpire vowed the same if he did it again. Grandfather was in the stands with my mother and me. *That's the way to do it, son,* the old man had shouted. *Show them we Matneys don't back down.*

Volatility, calculation, *and* a sense of superiority, and yet another element—desperation. What might my brother do at twenty-one if he believed Ligeia threatened the future he'd planned, especially the one with

Leslie. I think of the slit hose on the gas mask. A slit hose and a slit throat, the same in their effect. The Ka-Bar knife, which had weighted his right pocket since childhood, could have done it easily. But to imagine Bill's hand on the knife cutting Ligeia's throat, his face close to hers, as it would have to be, that *intimacy*, and then to watch her bleed out and after that bury her.

Another burial, not imagined but recalled. Nebo had not come to Grandfather's funeral, but he'd been at the cemetery, standing alone, dressed in the same mismatched work clothes he always wore. Perhaps like many of us there, he could believe Grandfather was truly dead only when dirt clods began thumping onto the coffin. Afterward, Nebo boarded the bus, no suitcase, nothing but the clothes on his back and whatever was in his pockets. He was never seen again. Months later when my mother and I were selling Grandfather's house and grounds, I ventured into the guesthouse where Nebo had lived for fifty-six years. It was as spartan as I'd expected, almost everything utilitarian. The only surprise was a heart-shaped locket left on a nightstand. Inside the locket was a black-and-white photograph of a young woman. Engraved on the back: *For my beloved Nebuchadnezzar.* Mother, girlfriend, sister?

Beloved.

So people surprise us. They can lie to each other, as my brother had done to me, and as I had lied to him that September evening at Panther Creek, and now it appeared those two lies could only lead to one imponderable truth.

That July I bought an AM/FM radio at Pike's Drugstore. Before, I'd spent the last hour awake reading or attempting poems and stories in a Blue Horse notebook, but now I spent much of that time with a finger and thumb on the dial, searching for stations playing the music Ligeia told me about. The signals drifted in and out between gulfs of static. After a while I knew where they'd be if they did break through. I'd imagine the pulsing antennas of Fort Wayne and Chicago, New Orleans and Kansas City. Even on the best stations, like WLS in Chicago or WKDA in Nashville, there would be top-forty fluff, but then I'd hear something by the Doors, or Jefferson Airplane, or Big Brother and the Holding Company, even an occasional single by the Dead or Jethro Tull. I learned to recognize bands by voices, Morrison or Joplin, or by guitar, Clapton or Hendrix.

I was already telling my mother I wanted a turntable with stereo speakers for Christmas. I made lists of albums to buy, groups I'd never heard of before Ligeia came. But in late July I'd found an even better station, not thousands of miles away but in the next county. Waynesville had a small FM station that played gospel and country all day and bubble-gum pop from seven to ten in the evenings. Except on Wednesday nights. Perhaps the station manager assumed that those who'd object were busy beneath the steeples dotting our region's every nook and cranny. But for whatever reason, it was as if someone had hijacked a minibus filled with albums bought in Haight-Ashbury, because the DJ had a penchant for album cuts from West Coast bands.

It was here I first heard the Grateful Dead's "China Cat Sunflower," and Quicksilver Messenger Service's "Light Your Windows," and the Steve Miller Band's "Children of the Future." But also darker tunes, including the darkest of them all, the Doors' "The End," with its premonition of what would soon come about in Brentwood and Altamont. Reflecting now on that summer, I realize the Doors were the group I should have listened to most intently.

In my freshman comp class at Wake Forest, I wrote an essay about listening to these stations and imagining the restless cities below their stilt-like towers, and how one day I would visit those cities, perhaps write about them. I remember my search for the right extended simile: the static like sand I sifted through

to find gold nuggets, the radio towers like light-
house beacons showing me the way to where, like
Wolfe, I could escape the "imprisoning" mountains.
The one I settled on was of bottles swept onto a de-
serted island by waves of sound, and in each one the
same message: *Swim away from the island and we'll
be out here to rescue you.* B+, my instructor wrote,
forgiving my purple prose and Shelleyan angst, but
not two misspelled words and a misplaced modifier.
*He was like a man who stands upon a hill above the
town he has left, yet does not say 'The town is near,'
but turns his eyes upon the distant soaring ranges,*
Thomas Wolfe declares at the end of *Look Homeward, Angel,* and those words I spoke aloud to the
bathroom mirror that summer, and thought of Wolfe
in New York, writing between journeys to the West,
and of Hemingway traveling from Paris cafés to Afri-
can veldts.

"You're the sweetest guy I've ever hung out with,"
Ligeia said two Sundays after Leslie's visit.

In her hands was the chain and small silver sea horse
I'd bought at Brock's Jewelry the day before. When
I asked if I could put it on her, she gathered her hair
and bared her neck. I kissed the pale white skin before
hooking the clasp.

"You're raring to go, aren't you?" she said, opening one of the three Quaalude packets I'd brought. "Soon as I eat my candy, I'll be ready too."

Afterward, we lay on our backs. The honeysuckle's sweet blooms thickened my languor. *There can be nothing better than this.* That's what I'd thought that afternoon, Calypso had come to Carolina. We sat up and finished the wine.

"That radio station I told you about," I said as I filled my cup, "the DJ played the Jimi Hendrix Experience."

"He's a great guitarist," Ligeia said. "Damn, I've got to at least get a transistor radio, because I'm marooned up here until October."

"For certain?"

"Yeah. My old man is still telling Uncle Hiram this place has been so good for me that I should stay for my senior year. Which is bullshit. They're just wanting to dump me off on someone else."

"I'm glad you'll still be around."

"Well, at least I found someone to help me make some money," Ligeia said. "Her name's Angie Well-beck. I met her in Sunday school. You know her?"

"I know who she is. She'll be a senior like you, right?"

"Yeah. Uncle Hiram and Aunt Cazzie like her parents since they're real churchy, so they're letting me hang out a couple of hours with Angie on Saturday. They think she's a good influence, but Angie's a wild child too, and she has wheels, so at least I can go somewhere besides church and the Dairy Queen. But the best thing is, Angie digs getting high, and she knows who else does too, including some who'd use the harder stuff I can get from Florida. From what Angie says, I can even make enough to buy some straight-looking clothes to interview in. That way I'll get on at a fancy restaurant where they tip big."

She paused.

"What's bumming you out?"

"I kind of hoped you'd want to stay here."

"If I don't return to the ocean I'll just die," Ligeia said. "But you can come visit and crash at my place. I bet you'd dig Miami. The ocean is right there, and they don't let it get scuzzy like at Daytona Beach."

"It sounds nice."

"By the way, Tanya had the book *Of Mice and Men*. She left it when she moved out and I read it."

"Did you like it?"

"It was good, except I didn't like how it ended, but that other book I'll skip," she said, and smiled. "Angels don't much interest me, if you haven't already noticed?"

"It's not really about angels. It's more about growing up."

"Then it's too late to do me any good," Ligeia said. "So writers make enough money to live on?"

"Some writers, but for others it's hard."

"I guess you don't have to worry about that though. Your grandfather will leave you plenty of dough, I bet, and that big house. All my parents will leave me and my sister will be some junky furniture and a beat-up truck. We rent our house, and it's so crummy I wouldn't want it if it was ours."

"I don't want my grandfather's house, and I don't want to live in Sylva."

"Where do you want to go?"

"A lot of writers live in Paris or New York; Thomas Wolfe did. I might for a little while, but after that some other place."

"Like where?"

"Ernest Hemingway lived in Key West," I said, trying not to blush, "maybe somewhere around there."

"Like Miami," Ligeia said, her smile widening. "That way you could hang out with your mermaid."

"I'd like that," I answered, "I'd like it a lot."

"And the book you write could have me in it."

"Definitely."

"You promise?"

"Of course."

"Well, promise me something else," Ligeia said, "that you'll leave out these freckles and give me eyes blue as the ocean, not the way it looks up close, but like in a photograph or painting. And change my first name into something that's not so lame and ordinary as the one I've got."

"Anything else?"

"And give me a happy ending," Ligeia said, her smile vanishing, "because it's not going to happen in real life."

"What makes you think that?" I asked.

"I don't think it. I know it."

We sat a few more minutes.

"I'd better go," she said, but instead of getting up, she placed her hand flat on my stomach and then slid it inside my jeans. "Unless you're ready to make it again. If you are, I can stay a bit longer. After all, last week you got all the attention."

"I didn't bring another, you know . . ."

"It should be safe," Ligeia said and stilled her hand. "But of course if you don't want to."

No, not once, I lied when Bill asked me two months later.

But I had.

PART THREE

CHAPTER THIRTEEN

Tell my brother I need to talk to him right now," I say, leaning close to the glass, "or I'm going back there myself."

"I'll tell him," the receptionist whispers harshly, "but he's with a patient."

"Like you told him earlier today when I called?"

"I *did* tell him, Mr. Matney."

"Let him know now," I say, my voice rising.

She presses a button and I expect a security guard to appear. But it's a nurse.

"Tell Dr. Matney his brother demands to see him," the receptionist says tersely.

The nurse disappears. Soon an elderly patient, back encased in a hard plastic shell, comes out and Bill follows.

As the patient steps to the receptionist's window, my brother motions me to his office.

"Don't bother sitting down," Bill says and closes the door, "especially if this is about Ligeia Mosely."

Bill stands next to me and I smell the Aqua Velva he still wears.

"You lied to me," I say. "You don't cut your own throat by *accident*."

It's not surprise, I think as I watch his face, but the resignation that something he'd hoped forgotten wasn't after all.

"How do you know that?"

"Robbie Loudermilk came to the house this morning," I answer. "He told me forensics found a cut on the front of Ligeia's spine. Damn it, her head was nearly cut off."

"Why would Robbie come and tell you that?"

"Angie Wellbeck, a girl at the high school, saw me give Ligeia money for the test."

"I can't talk about this now," Bill says. "I've got to prep for surgery."

"The hell you can't," I say, grabbing his arm. "This is more important."

"No, it's not," Bill says, his hand slowly but firmly removing mine. "There was a car wreck an hour ago. She's three years old and if I don't stabilize her spine she'll be paralyzed. So I can talk to you, or I can keep her from being in a wheelchair the rest of her life."

"Robbie Loudermilk may have time to talk to me," I say as Bill reaches for the doorknob.

"You're not going to see him."

"Why shouldn't I?"

"Because you have no idea what really happened."

"I know enough."

"No, you don't," Bill says softly. "You don't know anything, Eugene. I was there."

"Why should I believe you when you've already lied to me twice?"

"Because I lied for your sake, not my own."

I stare into eyes the same shape and color as mine, the one physical attribute we share. *But would you murder for your own sake, Bill?* I could ask, but shadowing that question is one for me: *Who caused her to be there that morning?*

"What if Loudermilk wants to talk to me again before you decide to unburden yourself?" I ask. "Angie gave him some names of guys who knew her. If they link her and us, he could be waiting for me at the house right now."

"Then don't go home. Robbie won't know where you are. I should be back by five. That's six hours I'm asking you for, Eugene. Six hours." Bill takes out his billfold and hands me three twenties. "Go get something to eat or some coffee, or go to Malaprop's and buy a book. But *don't* go home."

"I don't need the money."

"Just take it," he says.

I stuff the twenties in my pocket and we walk out.

"Maybe get here a few minutes before five," Bill says once we're on the sidewalk. "That way you won't be locked out if I'm late. I shouldn't be, but complications arise."

My brother strides across the archway that connects his office to the hospital. With six hours to kill, I'm in no hurry to get anywhere, so I leave my car in the office lot and walk down the sidewalk past the hospital, veer right, and enter the heart of Asheville's downtown. I turn onto North Market Street to pass Thomas Wolfe's house. I'd planned to do my dissertation on Wolfe. My advisor argued against it. Wolfe is all but forgotten now, she said, which seemed all the more reason to do it, so he would not be forgotten, or only, as Wolfe himself wrote, *by the wind grieved.*

The yellow house comes into view. A tourist stands in the yard, a camera strapped around his neck. When he sees me he turns and walks up the street. I step onto the porch. My mother had brought me here when I was fifteen, on a Sunday after I'd read *Look Homeward,*

Angel for the first time. She'd loved the novel, memo-rizing whole paragraphs, and, of course, naming me after the book's main character.

It is a novel you have to read as a young person or you don't get it. I've heard that said many times and it seems so. Like my mother, who'd read the book as a sophomore at Greensboro College, I discovered it at the right time. That day we walked through the house together, we'd discussed passages set in the different rooms, lastly in the upstairs bedroom where Wolfe's favorite brother died: *but who can believe in the noth-ingness of Ben?* "I never truly understood that passage until your father's death," my mother had told me as we stood there, her hand tightening on my arm as her eyes welled with tears.

I'm still on the porch when a man opens the door. He tells me the house is open if I wish to come in. I shake my head. That afternoon I'd visited here with my mother, a summer thunderstorm had come up and we'd waited on this porch until the rain and thunder ceased. She knew I wanted to be a writer and while we waited she'd turned to me.

"Isn't it amazing how you can go up to that room and see where Wolfe's brother died and then you can read about Ben's death in the book, dead in both life and in the book; and yet every time I reread and hear

Ben's voice, he's every bit as alive as before, and a part of me thinks this time maybe Ben *won't* die, and it hurts as much as the first time when he does."

I'd told my mother that I could understand that.

"I know you do, Eugene, and I know that you feel things as deeply in real life, and that can be hard, but look at it as a gift too. It makes us more fully alive, more human." My mother had paused. "The morning Bill left for Wake Forest, I told him that, if he were you, I would talk about how it was natural to feel homesick and lonely at first, even want to pack up and come back home, but that I didn't need to feel that way about him. I was trying to reassure your brother that he'd do fine away from home, but instead, for a moment at least, I believe I hurt his feelings. But then he said, 'Grandfather told me the same thing, so I'm certain I will be fine.' And of course Bill was. Almost a month passed before he called home."

"This is the last time William's getting beer and wine for us," I told Ligeia the last weekend in July. "He says it's not right, but I think it's because I can outdrink him. He can't stand not being the best at anything."

"What a jerk," Ligeia said.

"Yeah, I know."

"He's not drinking even one beer?" she asked, nodding at the plastic rings that held two beers as I pulled the tab off my fourth.

"No."

"If you have ten bucks I can score us some whiskey. Angie knows a bootlegger."

"I've got that much in my wallet," I answered. "I'll get it out of the truck before we leave."

"Good," she said. "You ever drunk whiskey before?"

"No."

"You'll live it, I mean *love* it," Ligeia said, and giggled. "Damn, it makes a difference taking three Quaaludes at once instead of two. Anyway, you'll get loaded quicker and you'll feel it sliding all the way down to your stomach."

"Sounds good," I said, holding up my can. "Three of these hardly give me a buzz anymore."

"Next time I'll bring that joint I promised you."

"Groovy," I said, trying to say the word without any hick accent. "How come you never smoke pot when you're here?"

"I don't need it with the downers and wine," Ligeia said. "I save the pot for other times."

She closed her eyes.

"Groovin' on a Sunday afternoon," she said, "right?"

"Right, groovin'."

"But not your brother."

"No," I answered. "He's still bitching about how loud my radio is. Says he can't concentrate. I told him to go buy some Geritol and earplugs and shut the fuck up."

She laughed.

"You really said that to him?"

"Pretty much," I said, "and guess what? Wednesday night I finally heard 'White Rabbit.' "

"It's the hippest song ever, don't you think?"

"Yeah," I said, propping up on an elbow, "and one by Moby Grape, though I didn't catch the title, and this new group, the Steve Miller Band. Have you heard them?"

"No, babe," Ligeia said, smiling drowsily. "You're going to be hipper than me before long. I bet you're already the coolest guy in this county, and once you start smoking pot . . . I bet you'll be trading in that pickup for a minibus by the time school starts."

Eyes still shut, Ligeia's hand found my forearm, lightly stroked the hairs with her index finger.

"Your mermaid needs a favor."

"What is it?"

"I need you to get me some uppers."

"You said you didn't like those."

"I don't, but other people do. I need some extra bread."

I looked through the foliage and caught a glimpse of Bill sitting by the big pool.

"I don't think that's a good idea. If you sell the samples, people could figure out where they came from. And Grandfather, he'll know if I take too much at one time."

"Six or eight tablets," Ligeia said, still stroking my arm. "Dexedrine or Desoxyn, okay? I'll take them out of the packets first. Hey, you know I'd do it for you. With a little help from our friends, that's how we all get by, right?"

"All right," I answered after a few moments.

"That's my babe," she said, and lay on her back again. "Thanks, Eugene, I mean it."

After a fourth beer, my worries began fading, and by the sixth, having taken some long swallows of Strawberry Hill, I was, for the first time, indisputably knee-walking drunk. The suffusing glow freed something inside me. *Freed,* though perhaps *summoned* is a more honest word. As I staggered upstream to get my wallet, Bill still sat by the pool. *He looks lonely,* I thought, *and that's a new feeling for him, like no longer being Grandfather's golden boy. And I'm glad he feels it.*

When Bill saw me he headed to the truck too.

"Back in a minute," I slurred as I took the ten from my billfold.

"What are you doing with the money?" Bill asked, but I ignored him and went on to the creek and gave Ligeia the ten.

"Don't forget the speed," she said, "as much as you can get, babe."

"And lions and tigers and bears, oh my," I giggled as she waded across the creek.

I fell twice before I got to the truck. As I came out of the laurel, I grinned at Bill.

"Lions and big brothers and bears, oh my," I said, and laughed so hard I fell again.

On the drive back, Bill didn't speak. Not that I gave him much chance to. I had the radio blasting, switching between top-forty stations for rock songs, banging the dash and singing along when I found "Light My Fire." We were nearly home when Bill turned into the post office lot and turned off the radio. He pulled a roll of mints from his pocket, took one for himself, and tossed them to me.

"Put the rest in your mouth, and sober up quick."

"Sure," I said.

As I loudly crunched the mints, the bright taste of peppermint filled my mouth. Bill didn't reach for the key. For some reason, the seriousness on his face brought to mind Elmer Fudd.

"Ehhh, what's up, doc?" I said, attempting a Bugs Bunny voice.

"I'm going to tell you some things, for your own good," Bill said. "This drinking, it's getting out of hand, and I talked to Tanya again. Ligeia didn't just use drugs, she got caught selling them. Prescription drugs, Eugene. That's serious. She was damn lucky she wasn't sent to reform school."

"So Ligeia's suddenly the worst person in the world."

"I'm not saying that, Eugene," my brother answered. "From what Tanya says, Ligeia's had it damn tough growing up. Her dad's never been able to keep a job and her mom sounds like a first-rate bitch. But that doesn't change the fact that she's gotten into serious trouble, and with people who weren't your age, or mine either. The guy she got arrested with was thirty."

"So you're saying what, William, that she couldn't like someone my age?"

"No, I just don't want you to get too involved with someone who could get you into serious trouble."

"You weren't worried about that in June."

"I didn't know as much then," Bill said. "If I had, I wouldn't have let us get involved with her in the first place."

"You can't stand it, can you?" I said.

"Stand what?"

"That Ligeia likes me, not you, that she doesn't give a damn about you having a letter jacket or planning to be a doctor."

"It's not about that at all, Eugene."

"I think it is."

My stomach roiled and a surge of bile rose into my throat but I held it down. I let my tongue rub bits of peppermint off my teeth to help dim the taste.

"I'm not taking you out there again," Bill said.

"Fine," I answered. "I'll take Mom's car. Ligeia can get us whiskey, so I don't need you to do a damn thing."

"You won't take Mom's car either."

"The hell I won't," I answered. "You can't stop me."

"But Mom will if she knows why you're going out there."

"And how much would you tell her about *us* being out there?" I replied. "You know, Bill, I can tell Leslie some things the next time she calls. I might beat you to the phone or maybe call Leslie myself, or write her a letter. Or maybe Ligeia and I can write a letter together. Ligeia might even mention that compared to me you're not even that good."

The truck's engine idled. I felt the vibration in the soles of my shoes. I knew my brother was waiting for me to tell him, Hey, I'm just kidding about Leslie, or maybe say that he was right and I shouldn't go to Panther Creek anymore. But I didn't say a word.

"Okay." Bill sighed. "But if you drive out there, you know you can't drink as much. If you were to get caught driving drunk . . ."

"Yeah, yeah, but just because you don't want a good time doesn't mean I can't have one, and that goes for Ligeia too, because I'm not afraid to get her what she likes."

"What do you mean by that?" Bill asked.

"Nothing," I said, realizing my mistake even in the alcohol haze. "I give her beads and stuff, and she likes them. That's all I mean."

I switched on the radio and turned up the volume. Bill waited a few more moments and then put the truck in gear. We drove on through town to the house. As we pulled into the driveway, he reached for my arm.

"You wouldn't do that, call Leslie or write her," he asked, "or let Ligeia know her address?"

"No, but like Ligeia says, I'm a lot better at screwing than you. That's something you'd better not let Leslie know, else she might decide to sleep on the couch with me next time she's here."

That will do it, I told myself as Bill's knuckles whitened on the steering wheel. Pain isn't so intense when you're drunk. That was my second thought.

"You're drunk," he said. "If you weren't . . ."

Bill got out of the truck and slammed the door. He didn't go into the house but started walking toward town. Afraid of what he might do to me if he lost control, or what I might do to him.

My mother was in the kitchen but I went straight to my bedroom, locked the door, and lay down, the bed wavering like a compass needle. When it finally steadied, I lay on my back and grinned at the ceiling. Then I spoke my thoughts out loud: *My brother is jealous of me. My brother is afraid of me.*

CHAPTER FOURTEEN

I take a left on Walnut Street, knowing this way I'll come to a coffee shop before a bar. My waitress wears the piercings and tattoos that are de rigueur for servers in Asheville. I face the window and sip my coffee, after a while order a sandwich. I've whittled an hour off my wait before I leave and walk to Pritchard Park. I watch a few not-so-covert drug deals, the drift of the homeless from one park corner to another, never venturing beyond. They resemble birds I saw once in a zoo, their only cage surrounding darkness, though here the darkness comes from within.

The long-term drunks are easily spotted—the gray-clay look of the drowned, short thin-ice steps learned from too many slips and falls. I guess which have a college education, once-promising careers. I pick out several, one because of his posture, another who acts ashamed he's here, and a third, who glares back at me contemptuously. *I know your story too*, his eyes seem to say, *and I find it tedious.*

Six months before the wreck, I was charged with drunk driving while returning from a bar in Waynesville. I'd worked out a ritual so as not to get caught— order a sixteen-ounce coffee with my last drink, to be more alert but also to cloak the whiskey. Chewing gum was a tip-off. The most important thing was to offset the alcohol by driving five miles under the speed limit, slower but not slow enough to draw attention. No radio or CD playing either. I focused between the center and roadside lines and looked at nothing else. It had worked until a traffic stop one night. The trooper asked me to take a Breathalyzer test and when I refused, a roadside test, which I thought, wrongly, I could pass.

Kay had called Bill and he'd paid my bail and brought me home. The three of us talked at the kitchen table while Sarah slept in her bedroom. An "intervention," that was the term just starting to be used for such conversations. Bill suggested AA meetings and Kay agreed. An overreaction, I argued, but promised no more drinking and driving and no more alcohol on weekdays. *If it happens again*, Kay said, *Sarah and I are leaving.*

So I'd learned my lesson. I drank at home and only on weekends, though weekends soon included Thursday and Sunday nights. One such evening Sarah was at a school play rehearsal. The director was sick and ended practice after thirty minutes. Kay's Sierra Club meeting wouldn't be finished until eight thirty. "I'm outside and it's cold, Dad," Sarah had complained. I got there fine, but Sarah wanted to talk about the play on the ride back. Maybe that was the difference, because a mile from home I didn't stay between the lines.

I only dislocated my shoulder, but Sarah's forehead was cut and her leg so badly broken a trooper blanched when he saw it. I watched as the medics inflated a plastic brace around the leg and carefully laid her onto a gurney. I told them to take her to Mission in Asheville, not Waynesville, and to have the hospital contact Dr. Matney. I kept demanding it even as the trooper snapped handcuffs on my wrists.

"You look like you might need something," a voice says.

A long-haired young man, probably still in his twenties, has left the park and sidled up beside me. Despite the day's warmth he wears a camo jacket. He opens the pocket closest to me and I see an amber-tinted prescription vial.

"No, thanks," I answer.

I turn and walk down to Malaprop's, browse the shelves to kill some time. I see a nice new edition of *You Can't Go Home Again* and open it, but I can't focus enough to make the splotches of ink have any meaning, so return the book to the shelf and walk back down Walnut Street. When I come to the Wolfe house, I step onto the porch and sit in one of the rocking chairs. I think of Thomas Wolfe and how he would have witnessed his older brother's body being brought onto this porch and down the steps. I wonder how Wolfe's portrait would differ if Ben had lived. What negative traits, so present in portrayals of his other siblings, might he have added?

I try to recall more about that late-September evening when my brother returned. He took a shower, but was it a long shower? Was there a residue of dirt, perhaps blood, on the shower tile or bathroom sink? And the next morning, scratches on his hands or neck if not on his face? What of Bill's pocketknife? Had it been replaced or "lost"? But if I'd once noticed such things, nothing remains. *Nothing but remains,* according to the newspaper. *S*uch appalling blankness in that word; even *bones* allows some visual connection, something that at least can be imagined.

I take the roundabout way back to Bill's office. It's a sunny day, so the street musicians are out, playing with varying degrees of competence everything from Earl Scruggs to Mozart. As I come up Church Street I pass a vintage record store. Music from Asheville's classic rock station plays inside. Some memories are heard before envisioned, so I sit on a bench and listen. The first song is too recent for me to recognize, then "Black Water" by the Doobie Brothers. It is the third song that triggers memory, not of Bill but of the afternoon Ligeia brought the joint.

"Hold the smoke in as long as you can," she'd said, and handed it to me.

I did what she said, trying not to cough. I drank from the pint of whiskey, one burn following another.

"Deep, babe," she said.

I took three more draws. Ligeia rubbed the ash off with a finger and relit what was left.

"Open your mouth," she said, and raised the joint, inhaled, then leaned so the smoke passed into my mouth. I held it in as long as I could and exhaled, the gray-white smoke suspended between us briefly before dissipating.

"That should get you off," Ligeia said, and nodded at the Quaalude and Dexedrine packets. "Thanks for getting all that for me."

She swallowed some whiskey and grimaced.

"It takes getting used to, doesn't it?"

"It's not so bad," I said, and, taking the bottle from her. I held the whiskey in my mouth a few moments and then swallowed. "Where does the bootlegger live?"

"You'll dig this," Ligeia said. "He's on the same road as the church Angie and me go to."

"Norman West Road?"

"Yeah, it's on the left, just a few houses before you get to the church. There's a silver horse trailer in the side yard."

"I'll get the whiskey next time," I said.

"And more of these?" Ligeia asked, nodding at the Dexedrine packets.

"Maybe I can get a couple," I answered, "but the Quaaludes and Valium, if I take any more of those . . ."

"Look for Librium then. It's downer too."

"All right," I answered.

"School starts two weeks from Monday, right?"

"Yeah."

"Good," Ligeia said. "I never thought I'd get my kicks at school but I'll be freer there than at Uncle Hiram's place. Aunt Cazzie hardly leaves the house except to buy groceries. I'm out in the barn every day, smoking up my profits, just to keep from going completely nuts. Speaking of which, do you feel that pot buzz yet?"

As soon as she said it, I did. Everything shifted closer and then farther away. *One pill makes you larger, and one pill makes you small,* I told myself, then said the words aloud.

"'And the ones that mother gives you don't do anything at all,'" Ligeia added. "That's a great song, isn't it?"

"Groovier than groovy," I said, grinning. "That show I listen to played it again last week. 'Feed your head.' That's how it ends."

"Yes, 'feed your head.'"

We chanted the words to each other, like a mantra, until Ligeia stood up and motioned toward the creek.

"Come on, let's get in the water."

I took another swallow of whiskey and stood. The world swirled around me. It was like a carousel ride, except I was on the carousel and watching it at the same time. On the bank Ligeia took off her bikini top and bottom. She waded in until her pale breasts bobbed. Unlike where Bill and I swam, this pool was surrounded with more laurel than trees. Sunlight dazzled the pool's surface and for a few moments I believed that Ligeia's lower body shimmered in silver scales, and that she was summoning me to follow her downstream, back to her magical ocean kingdom.

I removed my cutoffs and waded in, but the pool's wider sky brought with it a sensation of vulnerability. What I'd felt in June came back now, but more intensely. I knew I was being watched, if not by Grandfather then by a policeman or game warden. I looked upstream and Bill wasn't there. *No,* I thought. *He didn't come today, and it's because he knew what was going to happen.*

"What's wrong, babe?" Ligeia asked.

"Somebody's watching us," I said, splashing to the bank and jerking on my cutoffs. "They know we've got drugs and they're going to arrest us."

Ligeia came out of the water and we stood still and listened. The only sound was a woodpecker's *tap-tap-tap* near the road. No, I thought, it's not a woodpecker, it's someone using that sound as a signal.

"There's no one else here, Eugene," Ligeia said, holding my hand as she led me back to the quilt. "Lay down and close your eyes. Listen, babe, sometimes pot can do this. In a minute or two you'll be okay. I promise."

She settled behind me and placed her arm over my stomach and pulled closer, her bare breasts against my back, knees and thighs touching mine. After a few minutes I felt better, but I'd confirmed what I'd never doubt again, that despite all the songs celebrating pot, my drug was the old-fashioned one. And now I knew where I could get it for myself, and I would.

Feed your head, Grace Slick wails a last time and the final drum cymbal fades from inside the record store and the song is over. But then the song is not over, in my head at least, because a line of verse scalds like a cattle brand:

And the red queen's off with her head

CHAPTER FIFTEEN

When I look back on the summer of 1969, I marvel at how unconnected Sylva seemed from the rest of the United States. To young people raised on the Internet, it would be unimaginable. A boy from Sylva had been killed in Vietnam, another badly injured, but the war never felt *within* our world. Neither did the antiwar movement in Berkeley, the civil rights protests spilling into violence in Louisville and New York, or the killings of Sharon Tate and her friends in California. We saw these events on WLOS in Asheville, the sole TV station we could pick up, but drained to black and white and behind glass, it was if we peered into a telescope at some alien world.

So little changed in Sylva. As they had since my earliest memory, the same stores stood on Main Street, and what was inside varied little. The smallest things had their assigned place. If I went into Pike's Drugstore, candy bars were in front of the counter, comic books on a wire rack to the right. Winkler's Restaurant had the same menu year after year, the same food served on the same green plates. A few things might change, a new brand of sunglasses at Dodd's general store, some bell-bottom jeans at Harris Clothing, but these anomalies, like the first cracks in a house's foundation, went unnoticed.

A willed innocence masking the world's injustice and evil, even the town's name a nostalgic turning away from reality, some might say. There would be some truth in such a view, but Sylva's residents needn't look beyond their own town to know injustice and evil. As Sheriff Loudermilk noted, small towns have a way of giving up their secrets.

Some, however, are not given up, one of which was why Shirley had worked for my grandfather three decades when most of his nurses rarely lasted a year. She never questioned what he asked her to do, which included telling patients to their faces that Dr. Matney refused to treat them. She'd seen his temper, his bullying, and at times surely endured it, though strangely enough, I can't recall witnessing such a moment. Nor can I remember a single instance when she questioned what he asked or did. Even that one seeming act of defiance—stabbing the needle in her own arm—could be seen as an act of submission. The abuse of Bill and me hadn't been challenged, instead, partially absorbed. I do know that Shirley had eloped when still a teenager and returned to town five years later with a nursing degree but no wedding band. She'd moved back into the same house she'd fled and lived there with her mother, and when her mother died, Shirley lived there alone. What had happened during those five years was unknown. No one, including her parents, had received a phone call, telegram, or letter. I had been at her funeral, and the town gossips were still wondering. But the consequences of that return were clear. In a small Southern town during the 1950s, elopement and divorce were serious moral transgressions deserving of punishment. Maybe Shirley believed so too, and that Grandfather was that punishment.

When I awoke on Monday morning, I had to cover my head to avoid any piercing shard of light. Had I not felt so bad I'd have been more alert, because Bill watched me closely since my drunken "I'm not afraid to get her what she likes" comment. Grandfather and Bill were with a patient and Shirley on the phone when I went into the hall and opened the closet door. I stuffed a Librium packet into my pocket and was reaching for some Desoxyn when Bill's hand clamped my wrist.

"You come with me," he hissed, pulling me through the reception room and out the front door.

Bill was about to drag me into the side yard, but stopped when he heard the rasp of Nebo's razor.

"I'd hoped that was just drunken bluster," Bill said in a fierce whisper. "How many times have you gotten something out of there?"

"What's it to you?" I answered. "You did it."

"I did it once, *once*. How often, Eugene?"

"Take your hand off me," I said.

Bill did, but stayed close to keep his voice low.

"Tell me, damn it."

"Every week after the time you did it," I answered, rubbing my stinging wrist.

"Every week," Bill said, shaking his head. "What is wrong with you? I told you we couldn't do that."

"Maybe I'm tired of you making the rules."

"It's not about rules," Bill hissed. "If those packets get traced back to Grandfather's office, it won't be just him knowing, which is bad enough, the law will be involved."

"Don't get so bent out of shape," I said.

"Are you listening to me? If the SBI only *suspects* we are involved, our futures—"

"*Our* futures?" I interrupted. "Don't you mean yours? You're freaking out because you're scared it might keep you out of med school."

"Not could, would," Bill said, stepping closer, his face inches from mine. "I've worked my ass off at Wake Forest three years to get into Bowman Gray, and if you think I'm going to let anyone screw that up, you're wrong."

The office door opened and Shirley came out to tell Bill our grandfather needed him. He nodded and Shirley went back inside.

"Damn it, Eugene," my brother said, grasping my arm. "Don't do it again. Do you understand?"

"Sure, William," I said.

"You know, I've tried to be . . ."

Bill let go of my arm.

"But you will," he said resignedly, and went back into the office.

The next morning Grandfather stepped onto shattered glass when he entered his private office. A windowpane was broken and the paint chipped where someone had tried to jimmy the wooden frame. At lunchtime Nebo came in with a power drill and installed a Corbin brass padlock on the closet door.

"Even if some son of a bitch does break in, he's not getting into that closet," Grandfather told us and pocketed the key. "That's probably what it is, some welfare deadbeat stealing drugs. I hope he tries again, because Nebo's spending the night in here for a while."

"So you won't be able to get in the closet again?" Ligeia asked the following Sunday.

"He's got a lock on it and there's only one key."

She sat beside me on the quilt, hands clasped around her knees, the empty Quaalude packet beside the pint of whiskey I'd bought from the same bootlegger Angie used. He didn't know who I was, and when he asked I said a friend of Angie's, which was enough to elicit a grunt and disappearance into his house. He came back with a bottle and I paid him. *Don't you come at day-light no more,* he'd told me. *I ain't exactly selling you kids sno-cones.*

"But I can get plenty of this," I said, picking up the bottle and taking a swallow. "Next time I'll bring two pints. We can still get loaded."

Ligeia looked toward the stream, then spoke.

"I think it's a sign."

"What kind of sign?"

"A sign that summer's over," she answered. "Time for us to move on, right? It's been groovy, but 'ob-la-di ob-la-da life goes on.' Besides, Angie and her buddies are starting to help me deal. They're all seniors and when school starts next week I'll be hanging out with them."

"So this was just because I got you drugs?" I asked. I turned my head and stared at the creek. When Ligeia touched my shoulder, I slid out of reach, only then looking at her.

"No," Ligeia said, her blue eyes meeting mine. "Making it with you, it's been good. But you are just a kid."

"I'm just a year and a half younger than you."

"Only on a calendar, babe," Ligeia said.

She moved closer and kissed me on the mouth, a long, lingering kiss.

I reached to untie her top, but she took my hand away. I must have looked like I was about to cry, because then, very softly, she said, "Okay, one last time," and reached back and undid the ties herself.

I thought she might change her mind, so I went to Panther Creek at two o'clock the following Sunday. I sat by the pool and waited, the bootleg whiskey lowering in the bottle as did the sun in the darkening sky. It was my first time drinking alone and two epiphanies came to me. The first was that I was a tragic young swain fallen upon Shelley's "thorns of life." I outgrew that particular bit of sentimentality, but not the second epiphany: true intimacy with alcohol was best achieved alone.

Then school started back.

Ligeia's classes were mostly in the vocational wing, so I saw her only at her locker or during our overlapping lunch periods. Back then our high school allowed students to smoke as long as they did so on the grass outside the cafeteria. When I went to lunch the first day, Ligeia was outside with Angie Wellbeck and a couple of other girls, who, unlike Ligeia, wore heavy makeup. Their lipstick left pink rings around their cigarette butts. The rest of the smokers were males, the rough types who got suspended for cursing and fighting. They flicked burning matches at each other and threw elbows, their laughter aggressive, edged.

I sat where I could watch Ligeia through the cafeteria window. One of the guys came in and made a call on the pay phone. When he went back out, he and his buddies huddled with Ligeia and Angie. One of them saw me watching. He snuffed out his cigarette and came into the cafeteria.

"What the fuck are you looking at, asswipe?"

"Nothing," I mumbled.

"Well, sit over there," he said, shoving my tray to the opposite end, "and look at *nothing* from another direction."

I risked covert glances though, and lingered near her locker between classes. If she saw me, she smiled but didn't speak. On the Monday of our third week, however, Ligeia waited outside my homeroom. She looked worried.

"I need to talk to you," she said, and led me to a corner. "I'm still your favorite mermaid, right?"

"Yes," I answered, feeling a surge of hope.

"How about trying again to get me some speed?" Ligeia asked. "Maybe you can get the key or something."

"Grandfather carries the key in his pocket."

"Then maybe there are some samples somewhere else, like in his desk?"

"He locks it too."

"It's important," she said, greater urgency in her voice. "I think I'm in trouble."

"I can help you with money."

"How much?"

"I can get you fifty dollars."

"Fifty dollars won't get me out of this kind of trouble, Eugene. What about all that money in the bank? Isn't there some way you can get to it?"

"Grandfather has to co-sign. He'd make me tell him what it was for."

"You could lie," Ligeia said.

"No, he could tell if I was lying. Besides, he'd make it out as a check. Grandfather wouldn't give me cash.

But I can bring you fifty tomorrow, maybe even sixty. Won't that help some?"

"Bring it," Ligeia said, "but it's not nearly enough, babe. Not nearly."

It was only when the tardy bell rang that I understood what Ligeia was telling me.

Don't worry. It should be safe.

Should be, not will be, she'd told me that Sunday at Panther Creek. The Visible Man. That was the name of the human model Grandfather gave Bill and me one Christmas. Inside the clear-plastic exterior was a human heart with red arteries and blue veins branching out into head and torso. As my heart raced, it was as if I too were transparent, the blue and red strands wrapped like tentacles around my heart.

The bell rang for first period. I wasn't certain I could get up. *But she can take care of it,* I reassured myself. *That's what she was saying. It's just getting the money.* I opened my backpack, took out pen and paper and wrote "Are you sure about your 'trouble'? Maybe you are just late. Eugene." I folded the note and walked up the hall to Ligeia's locker and slid it in the door hinge.

At lunchtime Ligeia was waiting for me in front of the cafeteria.

"Yes, I'm sure, and you and Bill have to help me," she said, looking around to make sure no one heard. "He can get money out of his account, right?"

"Yes."

"How far away is his college?"

"Three hours."

"Call him and let him know," she said. "We'll meet at seven tonight, at the creek."

CHAPTER SIXTEEN

I return to the medical complex at 4:45. The receptionist doesn't send me back to Bill's office, so I sit
alone in the waiting room. Magazines cover the table
beside me. Most are what you expect in a doctor's office,
National Geographic, Sports Illustrated, that kind of
thing. Only one, *Christianity Today,* catches my eye.
I check the address label, and my brother's name, not
a patient's, is on it. Which shouldn't surprise me. Bill,
unlike me, has continued attending church as an adult.
Soon I may know what compels him to.

When I check the clock again it's 5:05, then 5:15,
then 5:20. *What if it's not surgery that is holding him
up,* I suddenly realize. Robbie Loudermilk may not
know where I am, but he could locate Bill easily enough.
Since this morning there might be new evidence,

or someone who'd seen the three of us at Panther Creek or noticed our truck there the day Ligeia vanished. Each thought solidifies into inevitability. I look down and see that my thumb and middle finger are pinching my left knee.

A TV is mounted on the upper corner of the far wall. It's turned to CNN, muted but with the closed captioning on. I go up to the window and ask for the remote. The receptionist looks at me and I know she's about to say something like *We don't allow the channel to be changed.* But we are alone and she knows Bill told me to wait, so she hands it to me without a word. Then, as if the remote were some acknowledgment of trust, she gathers her belongings, locks the front door, and leaves.

At five thirty I keep the television's sound muted but change the channel to WLOS. There's been a train derailment in Marion and a protest against the state legislature in Raleigh. After some advertisements, Sheriff Loudermilk appears. His words scroll across the screen, telling of a new source who claims Ligeia Mosely got behind on a drug debt and was eager to leave Sylva as quickly as possible. Which makes it more and more likely the murder was drug related, Loudermilk says, and a serial killer less likely. A third motive, the consequence of a personal relationship, has been considered too, the sheriff adds, but forensics has yet to find evidence of it.

"She sounded like it's real serious," I told my brother when he came to the dorm's hall phone.

"Serious for whom, Eugene?" Bill answered. "The way you've acted the last couple of months, I wouldn't—"

"She said serious for both of us," I interrupted.

"I've got my calc class this afternoon," Bill said. "You go and find out what this is about. Then call and tell me."

"Ligeia said both of us have to be there."

"If she's wanting me to get her alcohol or drugs, she can forget it," Bill said. "Where are you calling from, anyway? You're supposed to be at school."

"I am at school. I'm using the pay phone. You need to come, Bill. It's serious. I mean it."

"All right," he sighed. "Can you get out there without me having to pick you up?"

"I can use Mom's car."

"Good. I'd rather Grandfather not know I'm home in the middle of the week."

Bill and I got to Panther Creek first that evening. We sat down by the pool and waited.

"Where in the hell is she, Eugene?" Bill asked. "I've got a zoology test in the morning."

"I'm here," Ligeia said, stepping out of the woods, her shoes in her hands. She wore long jeans and a loose-fitting T-shirt with DISNEYLAND on the front.

"What is this about?" Bill asked tersely. "If it's drugs, you can forget it."

Ligeia looked at me.

"You didn't tell him?"

"Tell me what?" Bill said.

"That I'm pregnant."

Hearing the word aloud made everything, including the creek itself, seem to halt for a few moments. I'd feel a similar sensation the night of the wreck, the same time-distorting suspension between the car leaving the asphalt and the tree rushing straight into my headlights. Then, once again, I heard the creek, and slowly, like a carousel starting up, time resumed its normal pace.

"That's not possible," Bill said. "We were careful."

"Evidently not careful enough," Ligeia said.

"Look," Bill stammered, "if your period's a few days late that doesn't mean—"

"It's not a few days. I haven't had a period since mid-June."

"It could be something else."

I had seen this same hardness in her eyes before, but only for moments at a time. Now it locked into place like a dead bolt's click.

"Should I go see your grandfather to be certain?" Ligeia said. "We could all three go."

"No," Bill said quickly. "Just give me a minute to think."

He jerked his right shoulder, as if to throw off something that clung to him, then stared at the ground.

"Have you told anybody about this?" he asked, not looking up.

"No," Ligeia said.

"Good," Bill said. "Don't, okay?"

"All right," Ligeia said. "But I'm not dealing with this alone."

"I'm not asking you to. But a late period can happen for other reasons," Bill said, looking at me. "We were careful every time, right, Eugene?"

"Yes," I lied.

"One never burst or leaked, or anything like that?"

"No."

"Then everything's okay," Bill said, as if giving a medical diagnosis, "because nothing like that happened with me either."

"They don't always work," Ligeia said, raising a hand and splaying her fingers. "Maybe a fingernail pricked one, or something happened when it was made."

"I doubt that," Bill said. "Maybe . . ."

Then he hesitated.

"Maybe what?" she asked.

"Maybe," Bill said, "it was someone else."

For a few moments Ligeia look puzzled. Then she understood.

"How in God's name could there be?" she asked, her voice rising. "The only places I'd been was here or church. You damn well know it's true. I'm pregnant and I need money to do something about it. I need it *now*."

"Okay, okay," Bill said, raising a hand. "I'm just trying to get things clear. You can go to the Asheville Women's Clinic. They can do a pregnancy test. That way we'll know for certain."

"I don't need a damn pregnancy test. Just give me the money to take care of it."

Something shifted in Bill's eyes.

"No," he said, and there was no compromise in his voice. "Not until we're certain."

The wind gave a last sigh and grew still, the only sound now the gurgle of water.

"How am I going to get there," Ligeia asked, "especially if this is supposed to be such a secret?"

"I will take you if Bill can't," I offered.

"No," my brother said. "You can take the bus. The clinic is downtown, next to the courthouse."

"When?" Ligeia asked. "I can't just wait around, you know."

"In the morning," Bill said. "Once you get to school, walk down to the bus station instead. You can get back before school lets out. That way your uncle and aunt won't know."

"I'll need money for the ticket and the doctor," she said, "and for the test too."

Bill checked his billfold and took out two twenties and a ten. All I had was a five-dollar bill.

"How do I know this is enough?" she asked, taking the bills.

"I've got more at home," Bill said. "I'll get you at least a hundred. It shouldn't be nearly that much though."

"Worried I might not bring back your change?" Ligeia challenged.

"No, I'm just making sure you'll have enough. Eugene can give you the money at school in the morning. Then you can get on the bus."

"All right," Ligeia said, taking the bills from our hands. "But if I am pregnant, it will cost a lot more than a hundred."

"I know," Bill said, running the fingers of his right hand through his hair. He kept the hand on his neck and turned to me.

"If it comes to that, I'll get you the money."

"I'll pay half," I added.

"I'll pay it," Bill said sharply. "But none of us talks about this to anyone."

I met Ligeia in the parking lot the next morning, two more twenties and two fives clutched in my hand. Angie Wellback was talking to her. It didn't look like a happy conversation. Ligeia motioned for me to stay where I was. When Angie joined a group of girls nearby, Ligeia, hardly acknowledging me, came and took the bills from my hand.

Two days later after homeroom, she motioned me under the stairwell to avoid the rush of students.

"I called and got the results," she said. "I am pregnant, but the doctor told me since I wanted an abortion; she could arrange it, claim it was to save the mother's life. She got me an appointment at a clinic in Charlotte. She said they wouldn't hassle me."

"When?" I asked.

"Tomorrow afternoon at four thirty," Ligeia said. "I'll need money for a hotel and a bus ticket to Charlotte and then to Miami, because I'm headed there as soon as the doc in Charlotte says it's okay. I'll need fifteen hundred dollars. Tell Bill to bring it to the creek at nine tomorrow."

"How will you get to the bus station?"

"Bill can take me to the station in Sylva, unless he's scared someone will see him drop me off. If he is, we drive me to Asheville and I'll get the bus there."

"You won't be coming back?"

"Are you kidding?" she said incredulously. "Once I'm out of this place, it's forever."

"You told me you'd stay until October."

"No, I'm out of here," she answered as the tardy bell rang, "and don't look so sad. You knew I'd be leaving soon."

"I know."

"Be happy I'll be back where I belong."

"Yeah," I mumbled.

A last classroom door slammed shut and the hall lapsed into silence. Ligeia set her backpack on the floor, placed her hands around her neck, and took off the love beads I'd given her.

"Here," she said. "Something to remember me by."

I put the beads in my shirt pocket, then took a pencil and note card out of my backpack, wrote my address and phone number, and handed the paper to her.

"You'll write or call me when you get there, won't you?" I asked. "That way I'll know where you are."

"Sure," Ligeia said, stuffing the paper in her back pocket, "but it takes time to find a place and get settled, so it will probably be a while."

"Okay," I answered and paused. "You and I know this was my fault, not Bill's. I was the one that didn't wear the condom."

"No, we don't know that," she said, meeting my eyes. "I was certain it would be safe that day. It was safe. That's the truth, Eugene." She nodded at the empty hallway. "We'd better get to class."

"I really might come to Miami to live."

"Good," Ligeia said. "Look for a swanky bar or some white sand and you'll probably find me. Wouldn't that be a blast? And don't forget you promised to put your mermaid in a book."

"I won't forget," I said.

"And with a real cool name no one else would have," she added, "and blue eyes and no freckles, right?"

"Okay."

Ligeia gave my hand a soft pat.

"You had your own little summer of love, right?"

"I guess so," I said.

When she left, I went into the boy's bathroom, afraid that I might start crying. I told myself to be relieved, that the "trouble" that had sent me into such a panic was taken care of. I looked in the mirror. No tears. I took a deep breath and went on to class. I wanted to tell her one more thing, but it was too late.

"This will wipe out my checking account," Bill sighed later that afternoon.

"I want to pay half," I said. "I mean it."

"And what will you tell the old man so he'll co-sign?" Bill said. " 'Hey, Grandfather, Bill and I got this girl pregnant and we need money to pay for an abortion.' Yeah, that would go over real well, Eugene."

"I could pay you back a little at a time."

"No, I'm the one who will take care of this," Bill said. "The old man is right about one thing. You make bad choices and you pay for them. I did something stupid. So it's my responsibility, not yours."

"Because you're the big brother and you're supposed to look after the little brother, even when he doesn't want you to," I said. "Is that it?"

"Yes," Bill said, meeting my eyes, "and I will."

"I want to go with you tomorrow."

"No, you'll need to be at school," Bill said. "If you aren't and Grandfather finds out, he'll make you tell him where you've been. You know he wouldn't let up until you did."

I didn't answer but knew he was right.

"Ligeia said the procedure is tomorrow afternoon?" Bill asked. "That seems quick, but I suppose if the doctor says it has to be done right away, they make the accommodations. You're certain of that, tomorrow afternoon, not next Saturday?"

"Yes, damn it," I snapped. "Can't you believe I can do something right?"

"You haven't shown that lately," Bill said coldly, checking his watch. "I need to walk on up to the bank before they close."

The next evening Bill took Ligeia to the Asheville bus station. So that was it. Summer was over, and on the surface, Bill and I and the town appeared unchanged.

Ligeia's aunt and uncle filed a missing person's report, but she'd taken a packed suitcase with her so it was assumed she'd run away, probably to Florida, but as the sheriff had noted, what good was an out-of-state search when she'd be a legal adult in another month. It wasn't until Thanksgiving that I tried to talk to Bill about her. He'd placed a hand on my shoulder, then pressed so hard I winced.

"She got on a bus and that's it," he said, still gripping my shoulder. "Never ask me about her again. *Never.*"

At Christmas break, I ran into Bennie Mosely at the Shell station. I asked if his parents had heard from Ligeia.

"No, and that's fine by me," Bennie said. "Mom and Dad took her in and she left without a word of thanks. They even blame themselves for her running off, even though they were as good to her as could be. I hope I never see her again."

"What about her parents?" I'd asked. "Have they heard from her?"

"No," Bennie said, "and they're probably just as glad to be shed of her as everyone else. Aunt Ruth said that if she shows up in Daytona she'll not take her in. Aunt Ruth says she's eighteen, and for the rest of her life she's on her own."

CHAPTER SEVENTEEN

I t is after six when Bill comes in. He's clearly exhausted and doesn't speak as we go to his office. He sags back in his leather armchair and closes his eyes. I study the face of a man who's spent his afternoon cutting and probing the body of a child. For the best of reasons, of course, and yet . . .

"Another surgeon is going to join us in a minute," my brother says as his eyes open.

"Why?"

"Because you need to hear what he has to say."

"Not unless he was with you and Ligeia at Panther Creek that morning," I answer, "and if he comes in here with some bullshit that drugs caused her to cut her own throat, I'm going straight to Robbie Loudermilk."

"He's not going to do that," Bill says.

When a knocking comes at the front door, I shake my head.

"Tell him to go away," I say. "All we need to talk about is what happened, all of it."

Bill gets up and returns with a large, red-faced man. *Florid.* That's the best word to describe him. He's large, but a broad-shouldered large, perhaps a linebacker in high school, even college, though the hand he offers is soft. I guess him to be in his late fifties.

"Carl Bassinger," he says and sits down beside me. "I understand that you're skeptical about your brother's abilities as a neurosurgeon."

"I never said that."

"Oh?" Bassinger says, turning to Bill.

"Let's just say that my brother needs to know that what I do saves lives, or makes a life worth living," Bill says. "He needs to know how well I do my job."

"I'm on call tonight so I'll give the short version, Mr. Matney," Bassinger says. "I've been working at my profession for three decades and at four hospitals and your brother is the best neurosurgeon I've ever worked with. He's brilliant and he keeps up with the literature, even contributes to it, but that isn't what makes your brother truly special. Bill can do two things most of us can't. The first is that he can stay completely focused for hours. He doesn't start thinking about his golf game or some nurse's ass or his kid's soccer match. But what sets him apart most is the hand-eye coordination. That's something a surgeon can't learn; you're just born with it. Probably why he was a good baseball player," Bassinger adds, nodding at the photo of Bill in his uniform. "Same kind of thing. When you see Bill's surgery, his signature might as well be on it, because no one else's work is that clean."

Bassinger turns to Bill.

"What, eighteen years we've been together?"

"About that," Bill answers.

"Here's the thing laymen, or siblings, don't know, Mr. Matney," Bassinger says, giving me a wry smile, "and it's probably better that you don't. At every hospital there's usually one surgeon so ham-fisted you wouldn't want them cutting off a hangnail, much less poking around your spinal cord. And they don't care if they lock you in a wheelchair or not. They really don't, unless it results in a lawsuit. *Then* they care. As for the rest of us, we're competent and conscientious, but there's always one alpha surgeon. The nurses and anesthesiologists know who it is. Hell, the orderlies who wipe up the blood know. Bill's good enough to go anywhere, Mayo, Hopkins, but you mountain boys can't seem to leave home."

"Okay," I say. "I get that he's good."

"*Good*," Bassinger says. "Shit, *I'm* good. I've personally seen a dozen situations where paralysis or death were inevitable had Bill not done the cutting. Some surgeons wouldn't have dared make the attempt. Every surgeon makes mistakes, but Bill makes fewer. What your brother took on today, probably a fifty percent chance one of us would have botched it, but because he did it, that girl will walk again. You were damn lucky that when the orthopedist operated on your daughter— the one Bill got to fly back early from her vacation—he was in there with her. He made sure she did that surgery exactly right. Here's the thing. I've got three kids and five grandchildren. If one of them were rolled in with a spinal injury, I wouldn't do it. The scalpel would be in your brother's hand."

"How many good years do you think I have left?" Bill asks Bassinger.

"You're sixty-seven now, right?"

"Yes."

"Two or three more years for sure," Bassinger answers. "You'll be losing some coordination and vision, but the experience will balance that out for a while yet. When it doesn't, knowing you, you'll switch to pre-op and post-op care."

Bassinger nods at the picture of Bill and the Red Cross workers.

"I haven't mentioned how many people he's helped overseas. I don't know of a surgeon in this state who's gone on more foreign trips. You go every other September, right, Bill?"

"Yes," my brother answers.

"How many have you been on total, Bill?"

"Sixteen."

"Sixteen," Bassinger says, shaking his head. "I've been on two. Most surgeons go once and then for a week, if they ever go at all."

Bassinger checks his watch.

"Anything else you need confirmed, Mr. Matney?"

"Not from you," I answer.

"Okay then," Bassinger says, and stands.

"Thanks, Carl," Bill says.

"No problem," Bassinger answers. "You've had a hell of a long day, Bill. You ought to be home having a drink."

"Soon, I hope," Bill says, and they go out front together. They talk briefly, then the front door shuts.

"What does that have to do with anything?" I ask when Bill returns.

"Perspective on what occurred forty-six years ago at Panther Creek, and what has happened since, and can continue to happen."

"Something that occurred," I say. "That's a nice euphemism for a seventeen-year-old being murdered and then put in a hole and forgotten. God, Bill, you murdered her. You cut her throat."

"No, I didn't, but I bear responsibility."

"What in the hell does that mean? You killed her or you didn't. What happened, Bill, the truth. This time I'm not leaving."

"And you'll go to Loudermilk if I don't tell you?"

"Yes," I say, trying to sound more certain than I am.

"And if I tell you?"

"I can't know that until you do."

"Okay," Bill sighs. He pushes himself deeper in the chair and settles his hands on the armrest. "That afternoon when I went to the bank for the money, it almost emptied my account. Mr. Ashbrook didn't say anything to me but while his teller was getting the money from the vault, he called Grandfather, who told him not to give me a penny, so Ashbrook didn't. When I went outside, Nebo was waiting for me. He took me straight to the old man. Patients were there, but Grandfather took me to his office and shut the door. I made something up about moving my account to Wake Forest but he could tell I was lying. Then I said it was my money and I could do what I wanted to with it. You know how that went over. I finally told him the truth and of course he knew the scuttlebutt on Ligeia, and not just from her uncle. You know how Grandfather was. He knew about everything and everyone in town. He asked if Ligeia's uncle and aunt knew and I told him no, that she had promised not to tell anyone and I believed her. Then he came around the table and slapped me in the face, hard, and sat back down. For a while he just glared at me. Then he said hadn't I the sense to wear a condom and I told him I had, every time. Grandfather asked how I knew she was really pregnant, and I said she had gone to the clinic in Asheville. Then he told me he'd be the one paying Ligeia, and with his own money. The money in the bank was still mine but I'd better spend it wisely, he said, because I'd never get a penny more from him. Taking care of this mess was my inheritance," he said.

Bill pauses. An ambulance approaches the hospital, getting steadily louder. A wash of red light crosses Bill's window and then the siren shuts off. Bill closes his eyes a moment. The furrows in my brother's forehead deepen, as if the light and siren have triggered a migraine.

"Go on," I say.

"The next morning Grandfather told me to go out to Panther Creek first and park the truck where he'd see it. When he showed up, Nebo was with him. Maybe I should have realized something then, but you know he sometimes drove the old man places. When Ligeia asked for the money, Grandfather told her he'd called the women's clinic and said he was sending over a medical chart for Ligeia Mosely, but they told him they had no patient with that name. Ligeia claimed she'd used a fake name but Nebo grabbed her arms and jerked them behind her. Grandfather pulled up her T-shirt and prodded her stomach, then pushed his hand under her jeans and felt there too. He told me that I'd fallen for the oldest trick a bitch had." Bill's voice softens. "Maybe that would have been the end of it, but Ligeia said that even if she wasn't pregnant, she'd sold drugs his own grandson took from his office. If he didn't give her the money, she'd go to an SBI agent who'd been hassling her and her friends. She said she had empty sample packets to prove it. Grandfather looked at me and knew it was true. If Ligeia hadn't said that. If she just hadn't . . ."

"Nebo killed her?"

"Yes."

"While you just stood there and let it happen?"

"No. Grandfather sent me to get the money. He said it was in the Cadillac's front seat, but there was no money. I turned just as Nebo's right hand came around and brushed across her neck. It was so fast, like he was wiping off a bit of dirt. Then Nebo grabbed her by the hair and jerked her neck back and I saw the razor."

"Ligeia died right in front of you?"

"Yes."

"And you did nothing?"

"She'd fallen, so I kneeled beside her," Bill says. "I pressed my palm on her throat, trying to stanch the bleeding as I screamed at Grandfather to help me. I could stop it for a few moments, but there was so much blood. My hand, it kept slipping . . ."

Bill presses a palm over his eyes, leans forward so his elbow settles on the table.

"Then you and Nebo buried her and you all left?"

"Close enough to that."

"I don't want close enough, Bill."

"Nebo drove back to town to get two shovels."

"Grandfather didn't leave with Nebo?"

"No," Bill says, and looks up. "Nebo came back and wrapped her in a piece of tarp. We dug the grave and filled it, then covered the ground with leaves."

"You stripped off her clothes and her beads."

My brother nods.

"What did you do with them?"

"Nebo put them and the suitcase in the Cadillac's trunk."

"What did Nebo do with them?"

"Hell, I don't know, Eugene. All I know is that he put them in the trunk."

For a few moments, all is quiet. No words, no sirens in the distance, then a deeper quiet as the air-conditioning unit switches off. *Silence can be a place.* Those words come to me now. And it is where so much of my life has been lived, meaningless hours passed with the loudest sound the clink of ice cubes in a glass.

"Grandfather, he was a monster, wasn't he?"

"Yes," my brother answers. "He was."

"And you let him be one. You could have turned him in."

"When Nebo left to get the shovels, I told Grandfather I was going to the law, not Sheriff Lunsford but the sheriff in Asheville. He answered that it wouldn't matter because Nebo would take all the blame. He said Nebo couldn't speak but he could damn well nod his head and that was enough."

Please let me be dreaming this, I think, *or hallucinating in a hospital detox ward.* Another splash of red washes over the window, mute at first, then wailing as it leaves the hospital and heads downtown.

"You still could have told what really happened."

"Grandfather told me something else," Bill says. "He said he'd cut off every bit of money to Mom and you. He'd kick you out of the house."

And it's only now that I realize.

"You didn't tell him, did you?"

"Tell him what?"

"That I stole the drugs," I answer. "You didn't even tell him I'd ever been with Ligeia."

Bill shakes his head.

Why? I could ask, but I know the answer.

"How could Grandfather be so certain Ligeia wasn't pregnant?" I ask instead. "It was so early, and she could have used a fake name for the test."

"She wasn't pregnant," Bill says. "I'm positive about that."

I hesitate, then speak.

"There's something I never told you. One time I didn't use a condom. It could have happened then."

"I am telling you she was not pregnant," Bill says harshly, each word more emphatic than the last. "What's wrong with you, Eugene? Why are you wanting it to be worse than it already is? Isn't it terrible enough for you? You've read what the news said. She was desperate, she owed people money, dangerous people, and she'd have claimed or said anything to get it."

"No more dangerous than Nebo," I answer. "But even Nebo, how could he do that? He'd probably never even seen her before."

"Did you ever know him not to do what Grandfather asked?" Bill answers. "Can you remember *anyone* who didn't do what that bastard demanded?"

"You," I say, "when you married Leslie."

"What else could he do to me, Eugene? He'd already cut me out of his will. The last time I ever saw him, that Christmas when I told him to his face we were getting married, I lied to him. I said if he cut off your and Mom's money that Leslie's parents had money, a lot of money, and that they'd help Leslie and me but also you and Mom. I told him then everyone in Sylva would see that for all of his big talk about 'responsibility,' strangers had to take care of his own son's widow and child. That was the only lie I ever got past him. Over the years, I've thought about why he believed me. I think it was because he didn't care if people knew he was a murderer or a sadist or a blackmailer, but being viewed as irresponsible, that was the one thing he couldn't bear."

"I guess so," I reply. "But him not supporting Mom and me, kicking us out of the house, I'm not sure he'd have done that. He liked controlling us too much."

"We'll never know though, will we?" Bill says. "We'll never know about a lot of things. I mean, I can tell myself that I didn't go to the law because I was protecting you and Mom, but telling myself that is all I can do. I'll never really know. I had so much to lose, including med school, but most of all Leslie."

"Leslie may have stuck by you," I answer. "At the trial, I'd have said I was the one who stole the drugs."

"I stole them the first time, and even if Leslie did stand by me, how could I let her?" Bill says. "She'd know I'd been involved with Ligeia. She'd know I was there when she was murdered, and if Nebo nodded yes to *anything* Grandfather asked, wouldn't that include my being the one who'd killed her, or ordered Nebo to? It would be two testifying against one. And I did kill her. She wouldn't have died unless I'd caused her to be there that morning."

"I caused her to be there too," I say.

I look down at my hand and see a slight tremor. I haven't thought of a drink in hours but my body knows.

"Nebo's surely dead, and Grandfather's dead, and so are Ligeia's parents," Bill says, "and her sister and her aunt and uncle."

"How do you know that?"

"Because five years ago I checked."

Bill's desk phone rings. He reads the number but doesn't pick up.

"That's Leslie, wondering where I am," he says, and looks at me wearily. "I want to settle this once and for all and go home, Eugene."

"So Ligeia is murdered and no one's ever punished. It's all simply forgotten, again."

"Forgotten?" Bill says. "Every night when I'd cut off the light to sleep, I would think about her being out there in those woods. Every night. Every day."

Bill looks at me, seemingly about to tear up. I turn and nod at the Rembrandt print behind me.

"Grandfather willed you that because of what happened to her, didn't he?"

"Yes, and I'm glad he did. It needs to be there."

The phone rings again but Bill ignores it.

"What if Loudermilk or the SBI or forensics link us to what happened?"

"They won't," Bill says.

"She could have told another friend, or a relative?"

"She didn't," Bill answers and places a hand on his desk phone. "I need to let Leslie know I'll be home in a few minutes."

"You've lied to me twice about what happened," I say. "How do I know you're not lying now?"

"You don't," my brother responds, "but Carl Bassinger wasn't lying. This will all blow over in a few days. Except for you and me, it will be forgotten."

"And we do what?"

"We go on with our lives," Bill answers. "We live with it."

"What if I can't?"

"You will," my brother tells me. "Pour yourself a couple of drinks. If that doesn't help, consider the good that will come because you *do* live with it. Think what you want about me, think the very worst—that I want your silence solely because I don't want my life ruined. But think about what Bassinger said too."

"You still should have told me when it happened," I answer. "I'll never think otherwise."

Bill stares at me. When he speaks, the old familiar certainty is present in his voice.

"If I could have known how your life would turn out, Eugene, there would have been some mercy in having told you—it would have given you an excuse for the drinking and for everything else you've done to others and to yourself. But you didn't even have an excuse. You fucked up your life all on your own."

CHAPTER EIGHTEEN

I stop at the ABC store, getting inside just before the clerk hangs the CLOSED sign on the door. I pick out a fifth of Jack Daniel's, hand him the remaining cash Bill gave me, and pocket the change. I ache to fill the empty paper cup in the holder. To see the whiskey's amber glow is to be out in the cold looking through glass at a warm fire.

But I don't crack the seal until I'm home. As I sit down and take my first sip, my almost-memory of my father comes, the sensation of being lifted and rising above the faces of my mother and brother. To wave good night to the moon, Bill had told me. I don't remember my father saying that, or his face, or the moon, only the sensation of being carried, the weightlessness while moving from light into dark, adrift and unafraid.

No excuse, Bill claimed, and he's right, but if our father had lived . . .

I've just poured my second drink when there's a knock at the door.

"I've been calling your phone for the last two hours," Loudermilk says as he steps past me.

"I went to—"

Then I stop myself.

"You went where?" Loudermilk asks.

"Nowhere," I stammer. "Just out."

"Just out? Not to anywhere, just out?"

"Yes."

"You make a habit of acting skittish as hell every time I show up, Matney. I find that vexing."

Loudermilk walks over to the couch and sits down. He takes off his glasses and tugs his shirttail out enough to wipe the lenses, as if to say, *Yes, I've got all evening.*

"I checked out two of the guys Angie Wellbeck said Ligeia had drug dealings with, David Peeler and Tim Dickson. Did you know them in high school?"

"I knew who they were."

"Peeler claims that the last time he saw Ligeia she wanted to get away from here quick because she owed someone money. She didn't tell Peeler who, but she was real scared of what they might do to her. So what I want answered is whether Ligeia Mosely did or didn't get you the drugs you gave her money for?"

"I didn't give her any money."

"So Angie Wellbeck is lying about that?"

"Yes."

"No, she's not," Loudermilk says. "Angie told me to talk to Dawn Pinson. She saw you give Ligeia the money too."

"She's wrong as well, Sheriff."

Loudermilk's face reddens but his voice doesn't rise.

"Look, Matney," he says. "Can't you just admit you bought the drugs and tell me about the other people that girl knew? Like I said, I can't do a damn thing about you buying or selling drugs forty-six years ago. You did it and got away with it, just like you've gotten away with everything else in your worthless life. Do I need the Supreme Court to come and explain the statute of limitations to you? Are you that alcohol addled? All I care about is that the girl sold drugs and that's probably why she's dead. You damn well know something you're not telling me. She was involved with some serious dealers in Daytona Beach. One may have come up here, and if you know anything about him—description, name, nickname—give it to me." Loudermilk pauses. "Is it that you're afraid of who did it, that after forty-six years they're going to come after you and cut your throat? Are you that much of a coward on top of everything else?"

Loudermilk raises a forefinger and presses his glasses closer to the bridge of his nose. The finger slides slowly up on his brow, stops there briefly, as if probing for a thought. He leans back deeper into the couch and sighs.

"I knew her aunt and uncle, and they were fine people. I even went out with Tanya for a while when we were in high school. Ligeia was no saint, but she didn't deserve what happened to her, and I know that girl's disappearance caused her uncle and aunt a lot of guilt and pain. I know that for a fact, because I talked to Tanya yesterday. She said it tore her parents up, especially her dad, because his younger brother trusted him to take care of her. It was a *responsibility*. So here's the thing, Matney. Can't you do one responsible thing in your whole miserable life? Look, whoever killed that girl has gotten away with it all this time. They may be dead now, probably are, but at least we can show that Ligeia Mosely mattered enough to try and find out who cut her throat and left her out there to rot. Don't we owe her that?"

Loudermilk's shoulder mic crackles and a voice asks if everything is all right.

"Yes, everything's fine. I'll be out there in a bit," Loudermilk says, leaning toward the mic, before turning back to me. "So tell me, Matney. Don't we owe her that?"

"I've told you what I know," I answer. "I don't want to talk about this anymore."

"Would you be willing to take a polygraph test? Peeler and Dickson said they would."

"I don't think—"

But Loudermilk suddenly is not listening to me.

"Is this about protecting someone you know, someone still alive?" Loudermilk says, each word sounding less like a question and more like an accusation. "That's it, isn't it?"

"Before I admit anything," I answer, "I want to finish my drink."

"How many have you already had?"

"One. If I finish this one I'll still be sober."

"Finish it," he says.

I go to the table and lift the glass, slowly swallow, and set the glass down. I cross the room and sit in the chair across from Loudermilk.

"Wait," he says, and takes a card from his billfold. He reads me my rights and asks me if I understand.

"I understand."

"Go ahead."

"I killed Ligeia Mosely."

When Loudermilk speaks, it's ever so soft and slow, as if he might startle me into silence.

"You killed her? Ligeia Mosely, *you* killed Ligeia Mosely?"

"Yes," I answer. "If you want me to sign a confession I'm ready to do it. We can go now."

I set my hands on the chair's arms but Loudermilk nods at the Jack Daniel's bottle.

"Two drinks, that's all?"

"Yes."

"I will give you a Breathalyzer test as soon as we're at the station," he says. "I'm making sure your brother and his hotshot lawyer can't get you out of this."

"Go ahead, Sheriff. I'll pass this one."

"Okay," Loudermilk says, "and I'll dot every *i* this time. We're doing it at the station, and I'll have witnesses."

But Loudermilk doesn't stand. He is studying me, perhaps searching for signs of drunkenness or insanity, or relief.

"Why did you do it?" he asks.

"Angie Wellbeck was right," I answer. "The money I gave Ligeia was for drugs but she didn't me get the drugs."

"You killed her because she owed you money?"

"Yes."

"By yourself?" Loudermilk asks. "No one else was there?"

"I was by myself," I answer. "No one was ever involved except her and me."

"And you'll go with me to the courthouse and sign a statement saying that?"

"Yes."

"What about an attorney? You don't want one?"

"No," I answer, and stand. "I'm ready to go, right now."

"All right," Loudermilk says, and nods at the bottle. "So killing Ligeia Mosely, is that your excuse for being a drunk, knowing all these years what you'd done, knowing that she was still out in those woods?"

"No," I answer. "I have no excuse for that."

"No excuse," Loudermilk says, then says it aloud again, as if to commit the words to memory.

As he stands he carefully tucks his shirt into his pants and centers his belt buckle, perhaps already preparing for the press conference.

"You got any kind of weapon on you?"

"No."

"You'd better lock up the house," Loudermilk says. "You may not be back for a while."

I get my key and we walk out to the porch. Across the way I see a deputy smoking a cigarette as he leans against the squad car. Loudermilk gestures to him as I close the door. I turn the key and hear the click.

"Are you going to handcuff me?"

"Do I need to?" Loudermilk asks.

"No."

We go down the steps and the deputy opens the back door and I get in.

CHAPTER NINETEEN

I did try to leave that one time," my mother told me, her words punctuated by the beeps and hisses of the hospital machinery. "It was the summer when you were seven and Bill twelve. I knew it would be hard to support myself and two children but I felt we could get by. I sent out résumés to high schools and actually had an interview scheduled in Raleigh. But your grandfather found out. One afternoon when you and Bill were at the rec center, he came to the house with Sheriff Lunsford and Mr. Ashbrook from the bank. I thought at first something had happened to you or your brother. I was so frightened and kept asking over and over if you both were all right. Sheriff Lunsford had to tell me twice before it sank in that you and Bill were fine.

"They came in and we all sat down. Your grandfather said *Show her the check,* and the sheriff did. Your
grandfather had written it to me for a hundred dollars,
but now the one was a nine. The change was crudely
obvious. When I asked what this was about, the sheriff replied forgery, and that Mr. Ashbrook was ready
to testify that he'd personally taken the altered check
from me.

"*Only if I decide to press charges, of course,* your
grandfather said. He told me if I tried to leave Sylva
that he would do just that. I knew that he had me, and
everyone in the room knew it too. It's strange what you
notice in moments like that, a small something that you
later find significant. Your grandfather wore his suit despite the heat, and he noticed a piece of lint and picked
it off his pants and flicked it onto the floor. It was as if
my finally finding the courage to make a new life for
us elsewhere was no more difficult for him to deal with
than that piece of lint. There he was, two of the most
powerful men in Sylva beside him, and they were doing
exactly what he wanted. So I promised your grandfather that I would stay. *And never try to leave again,
correct?* he said, and I answered yes. I could tell Sheriff
Lunsford and Mr. Ashbrook were ready to leave, but
they didn't dare get up or even clear their throats. The
sheriff handed the check to your grandfather. But in-

stead of tearing it up he looked at me and said *But of course I may go ahead and put you in prison anyway, raise those two boys myself.* And for a minute no one said a word. The four of us sat there, Sheriff Lunsford, Mr. Ashbrook, and your grandfather just letting that threat linger, like his words were something he could taste and savor.

"Then Mr. Ashbrook spoke for the first time since they'd come. *If you try to do that, Dr. Matney,* he said, *I will not testify.* Some people might think his doing that was a small thing, but anybody who knew your grandfather would know otherwise, because Mr. Ashbrook had a family too, and I am sure sometime later he paid dearly for those words. Your grandfather didn't acknowledge what Mr. Ashbrook said, and I wondered if I'd really heard it, because Mr. Ashbrook had always seemed a milquetoast, more like a teller than a bank manager, the kind of man who'd faint dead away if a robber came in demanding cash. But then your grandfather had smiled, not at Mr. Ashbrook but at me, and said, *What would I do with two boys causing a racket around my house.* Then your grandfather stood and the three of them left."

That story is what I remember as I wait in the interrogation room, the Breathalyzer taken and passed, the sheriff and his witnesses, a clerk and a deputy, watching everything that is said and done. All that remains is my signature on the confession being typed and run off. A question enters my mind about the morning Bill tried to withdraw his money. If Mr. Ashbrook had known what it would lead to, would he have defied my grandfather a second time?

Maybe once is enough, I tell myself as I stand in front of the room's one window. At the end of the long gray hallway is the holding cell. I don't recall what it looked like inside. What lingers in my memory is the metal door clanging shut like an audible slap in the face. I sit back down and stare at my hands, wishing I'd bargained for one more drink. Or maybe it's better this way, let the punishment begin. No longer the Eugene Gant who sought escape, but instead Raskolnikov, who embraces his incarceration. But that romantic notion quickly dissipates with the thought of being gang-raped while stone-cold sober. For a moment I waver.

Sheriff Loudermilk comes in with the confession. He sits down but the deputy and clerk stand. The clerk's face is familiar, perhaps someone I went to high school with, because we look about the same age. Then I know her name and the knowledge is strangely comforting. Phrases come to mind: The theory of a unified field. The love that ended yesterday in Texas. Jungian archetype . . . All portend that this should be the right ending because it *coheres.*

"You're Renee Brock, aren't you?" I ask.

"Now it's Clark," she answers tersely.

"I bought a necklace at your father's jewelry store once. A silver sea horse was on the chain."

So what? her face says. As she turns to look out the window, hollowness is all I feel.

"This is being recorded," Loudermilk tells me, and nods at the camera in the upper corner. "One more time, Matney. You've been read your rights, and you've said you don't want a lawyer present, correct?"

I nod.

"Answer verbally."

"That's correct," I say.

"And by signing this confession you're admitting you killed Ligeia Mosely on September 15, 1969."

"Yes."

"Say it louder."

"Yes," I say.

He sets the paper and pen in front of me and I pick up the pen with my left hand.

Loudermilk reaches across the table and sets a splayed palm on the paper.

"Put the pen down."

"Why?"

"Where on her body was there a second cut?" he asks.

"What?"

"The second wound, where was it, you son of a bitch?"

I try to read Loudermilk's face to see if he is trying to trick me, but it's as if his features—eyes, mouth, forehead—are tightening like an animal preparing for ambush.

"Where was it, Matney?" he says again, loud enough that his deputy starts walking toward us. "Where else was Ligeia Mosely cut?"

"I know what you're doing," I answer. "There wasn't a second wound."

Loudermilk turns to his deputy.

"Cut off that damn camera," he barks, and turns to Renee. "Go on back to your desk."

When the deputy returns and confirms the camera's off, Loudermilk leaves his chair. He comes around the table and stands beside me.

"Get up," he says.

When I do, Loudermilk grabs my collar. He shoves me against the wall, his forearm pressed under my chin.

"What in the name of God is wrong with you?" he asks.

"There was only one cut," I gasp, and he presses harder.

"The hell there was, you left-handed son of a bitch," Loudermilk shouts. "They found a blade mark on her right pubic bone, the *inside* of the bone."

The deputy settles his hand on Loudermilk's shoulder.

"Sheriff," he says. "The window is open."

Loudermilk lets me go, takes a step back.

I bend over, heaving for breath.

"I—"

He leans closer. I can smell his hair oil, the mouthwash on his breath.

"Don't speak until I tell you to, Matney, or I'll beat you to a bloody pulp even if it costs me my job and whatever lawsuit your brother hits me with."

Loudermilk waits a moment, then lets go and steps back.

"So he wasn't even there," the deputy says, "much less killed her."

"No," Loudermilk says. "This sick son of a bitch doesn't know a damn thing, except how to drain a whiskey bottle."

"He can't even give you a name or two?" the deputy asks.

Loudermilk pauses. It's like he's seen a twitch on a fishing line.

"I'm going to ask you one more question, Matney, and I want a one-word answer. One word. I'll know if you're lying, so don't even try. Don't *dare* try. Do you know who killed Ligeia Mosely? One word, yes or no."

I meet his eyes.

"No," I answer.

For a few moments Loudermilk makes no reaction. Then he nods at the deputy.

"Go get his stuff from the cage."

"Yes, sir," the deputy says and leaves.

"I hope that the next time I see you," Loudermilk tells me, "your car is wrapped around a telephone pole, a single-car accident. If you're broken up bad, I'll tell the ambulance driver to drive slow, and to Waynesville, not Asheville. I'll not give your brother another chance to save your worthless ass."

He opens the door.

"Get out of here," he says.

As the deputy drives me home, I think of what my mother said about noticing something seemingly trivial at the time and yet, later, it proves important, definitive. What I remember was not at Panther Creek but at school between classes. Ligeia was reaching into her locker and one of the books crooked in her arm slid free and, as she made a fumbling gesture to keep it from falling, her other books spilled onto the floor.

She'd kneeled to gather them, her brown eyes looking up, the freckles darkening as her face reddened in
embarrassment. It is an unremarkable memory of an
unremarkable moment, something that happened to
everyone during high school. Just something human.

CHAPTER TWENTY

There was a last, brief newspaper article in which Sheriff Loudermilk stated that though Ligeia Mosely's death may well have been drug related, no solid leads had turned up. She could have simply walked the mile down to the interstate to hitchhike, her first ride her last. He conceded that the likelihood of finding her murderer was diminishing. Too much time had passed.

Nevertheless, for months I kept expecting someone to come forward and say Ligeia had mentioned meeting Bill and me on Sundays at Panther Creek, or else recalling our truck being parked there. But neither has happened and now it is winter. The earth around Panther Creek is buried beneath a foot of snow, the creek glassed by ice. No leaves remain to give the wind a voice.

Bill and I have not spoken again about her. It is in my brother's hands now, what good might come from what happened. I have almost finished with this story, and so my days will be emptier, the clock crawling toward five o'clock. Soon I will build a fire and when five o'clock comes I will raise my goblet toward the hearth and see through glass the refracted flames. As the bottle of whiskey empties, I may even see myself as a man who helps save lives, a spectral assistant each time the blade enters.

As for Ligeia, I have given her the exotic name and blue eyes and clear complexion I promised that afternoon on Panther Creek. Now, as the earth turns these mountains west into darkness, a final promise remains before I offer this story to the fire one page at a time. Fire and water. So now I write the ending, which happens this evening, not in this house or at Panther Creek or in my brother's office, but instead on a beach in Florida. A woman is walking barefoot, the incoming tide swishing over her feet. Her beach house is fifty yards farther down the shore. It is almost dusk and she sees the warm yellow light behind the panes. A man is there, finishing a final paragraph before he comes to join her. She feels a surge of happiness as she thinks how lucky she's been to survive her wayward years. Their daughter, grown now, will come to visit tomorrow and stay for a week. She will come back here in the morning and she and her daughter will hold hands as they enter the water together. Or perhaps there is no daughter come to visit, no husband finishing a story, or even a story—only herself, smiling as she leaves the sand and enters the ocean. She rises once, glances toward shore, then turns and disappears, a mermaid finally home.

Acknowledgments

Thanks to Kathy Brewer, Tom Rash, Bill Koon, Megan Lynch, Phil Moore, Marly Rusoff. Ann, Caroline, and James.

Onward.

HARPER LUXE

THE NEW LUXURY IN READING

We hope you enjoyed reading
our new, comfortable print size and found it
an experience you would like to repeat.

Well – you're in luck!

HarperLuxe offers the finest in fiction and
nonfiction books in this same larger print size and
paperback format. Light and easy to read, HarperLuxe
paperbacks are for book lovers who want to see
what they are reading without the strain.

For a full listing of titles and
new releases to come, please visit our website:

www.HarperLuxe.com

9